REBEL GUARDIANS

MOTORCYCLE CLUB

BRAXTON

LIBERTY PARKER &
DARLENE TALLMAN

COPYRIGHT

Braxton
Rebel Guardians MC Novel
Copyright © Liberty Parker
& Darlene Tallman 2018
Published by Liberty Parker
& Darlene Tallman
Cover by: Dark Water Covers
https://goo.gl/mhVY1Y
Edited by: Joanne Dearman, Kat Beecham, Melanie
Grey, Jenni Belanger, Darlene Tallman
Formatting by: Liberty Parker

DEDICATION

So, you get to read TWO of these—one from each of us. Aren't you the lucky ones? Anyhow, I had the privilege and pleasure of meeting Liberty and her sister, Kayce, at Wanderlust in Dallas in May 2017 and had an absolute blast. I felt like I had known them "forever", something that was obvious from the way we just clicked, you know? Plus, I've talked to Kayce multiple times this past year by phone, and Liberty by phone and messenger. Well, I drove from Georgia to Dallas and back home again and while driving home, it occurred to me that the three of us should collaborate on a series. Since they predominantly write MC (although I have three MC books right now), that's where my mind drifted. And of course, a muse started talking. When I asked the two of them, they were all for it. Right now, Kayce has other projects, so this first book is mine and Liberty's baby. We are beyond excited to bring the Rebel Guardians MC to life for you, our readers and fans. We're going to write through a program that allows each of us to tinker with the story so that you get a seamless read (if that makes sense). So, this dedication is to two more ladies in #MyTribe— Kayce and Liberty—who have believed in me from the word go and whose encouragement has kept me going on those dark, ugly days!

~ Darlene

To most writers this is the hardest part of any book...I'm no different it seems. There are a lot of important people in my life that pave the way for me in this industry. For this book I'd like to dedicate it to a couple of people. I know it's not the norm, but neither am I. First up is Tracie Douglas with Dark Water Covers, she takes our ideas and turns them into masterpieces. She's patient, kind and loves all of her authors equally, and that's really hard to find these days. Second up is my partner in crime Darlene Tallman, you have become my rock and one of my closest confidants. Thank you for the honor of requesting I co-author this book with you. It is one of the *most* fun experiences I've had, and it renewed my love of writing. So thank you my dearest friend.

~Liberty

ACKNOWLEDGEMENTS

We both would like to give a special recognition to Daverba Ortiz for all the promotional work you've done for Braxton...there are no words to show our appreciation.

The two of us have different beta readers (although some ARE the same). For me, I have to acknowledge them; they've been with me since "Bountiful Harvest" and their insight, suggestions, and edits keep my books flowing and making sense. Without them, there would be no "me" as an author. And, for one of the best cover designers out there who we all adore, Tracie Douglas, who takes what we are envisioning and makes it reality. You make us all look fabulous!

For my PAs—Vicky and Jenni—y'all can be quite...bossy at times, but I love y'all anyway!

For my dad, who slipped his earthly bonds at the end of 2017—Dad, your words that day saying you were proud of me? I will never forget them. Ever. I am and will always be proud to be your daughter. Now you and Mom can watch from above as I chase the stars. "You followed a dream and made it reality"—this could become a tattoo.

I also want to thank all of the ladies in #MyTribe as well as the readers who share our stuff "everywhere"! It doesn't go unnoticed, trust me, and the fact you want to read what I write is still extremely humbling. Thank you doesn't feel like enough sometimes.

~ Darlene

I want to first of thank my wonderful bossy PA Vicky Deviney Chelsey who's faith in me never waivers. She encourages me every day and is one of my biggest supports. Jenni Copeland Belanger who has recently joined the team I want to thank you for taking a chance on us and we've enjoyed you helping out wherever you've been able to. She's been very ill...get better soon sweetie, we miss you.

My Liberty's Luscious Ladies, you take my quirks and run with them. Always available for opinions, encouraging me to take new adventures and loyal to a fault. Thank you for joining me and being an ear when I need one.

To my husband Greg and my three boys Colton, John and Thomas. My life would be incomplete without you all at my back. My love for each of you is unwavering and unconditional. You each light my life in your own way, I love you <3

To my sister Kayce, always my back bone and one of my best friends.

To my mother Cheryl, there are no words in the written language to express my love for you. All I can say is, I love you Momma.

To my readers, my dream wouldn't exist without you. There is no greater joy in my life than

7

reading the reviews you leave letting me know how much my stories mean to you. If I can touch even one person's life I feel like I've fulfilled my purpose with each and every release.

<3#MyTribe: you know who you are.

~Liberty

AUTHOR'S NOTES

Braxton is a labor of love for the two of us and we have spent hours on the phone talking while we plotted as we went. We may or may not share a brain...but we'll never tell!

You may have questions...just know that "all will be revealed to she who waits" ...there are more books coming!

This book is intended for mature audiences 18 and older due to adult content

BOOK CHARACTERS

<u>Rebel Guardians MC</u>
Braxton *Axe* - President
Twisted - VP
Bandit - IT
Law - Club Attorney
Chief - SAA
Hatchet - Enforcer
Capone - Road Captain
Smokey - Secretary
Duke - Patch
Chef - Patch

<u>Prospects</u>
Chet
Boothe
Jaxson
Maxum

<u>Women</u>
Caraleigh
Nan
Donna Jo *DJ*
Paisley
Starla

<u>Kids</u>

Luca
Lily
Ralynn
Tig

<u>MC Businesses</u>
Rebel Guardians Transportation
Rebel Townhomes

TABLE OF CONTENTS

SYNOPSIS

The challenges of setting up a new MC were huge, but Braxton Callahan knew the rewards would be worth the hard work that he and his brothers were putting in. Relocating to Corinth, Texas had been interesting to say the least, but they wanted to live in a town where the businesses they were starting would help revitalize the area. A single father to Lily, a precocious six-year old, he longed to find the woman who would complete his family.

When Caraleigh Jensen moves in next door with her little boy Luca, who is the same age as Lily, he finds himself drawn to the widowed single mother.

Change isn't always bad and it isn't always good. Follow along as Braxton and his brothers continue to rebuild the town while he works to woo the woman his heart says is his.

PROLOGUE

Braxton

I sigh as I pull my cab into the specially-built garage next to the townhouse. While we are working to get more brothers licensed with their CDLs, I am doing the bulk of the long-distance runs. I smile as I think about the first business we started as a club—Rebel Guardians Transportation. We do long, and short-haul runs, transporting everything from fruits and vegetables to medical equipment and motorcycle parts. *I hate that I'm away from Lily so much.* That's probably the hardest part—she spends more time with her grandmother than me lately, something I hope will change sometime in the near future.

Locking the cab up, I realize that someone will have to take me to the office tomorrow to get my bike. I could drive my truck, but it's too nice outside. I usually bring my bike home, but the late hour had me rethinking that since I know how loud my pipes are. *Oh well, tomorrow is another day.*

Walking into the house, I notice a note from my mother—*Brax, I know you'll be getting in late. I'll take Lily to school in the morning. You need your rest. Love, Mom.* She has been my rock for more years than I can count. When Daria abandoned Lily as a newborn, I had just been freshly out of the Marines and clueless when it came to dealing with babies. My mom, a widow herself, had moved in and shown me the ropes, never taking over except when I was out on a run. *Time to do something special for her.*

Once upstairs, I check on Lily, quietly covering her back up and tucking her doll in next to her. Kissing her forehead, I whisper, "I love you," and creep back out, closing her door softly. I know that even if my mom is going to take her to school, she will still come bouncing in to see me once she realizes I am home. Going into the master bedroom, I head straight to the bathroom and take a long hot shower to wash the road grime away. *Damn, I'm lonely. What I wouldn't give to have someone to curl up with when I go to bed.* Someday. Now that I'm clean, it's time to make something to eat.

CHAPTER ONE

Caraleigh

I look around at my new place and grin. *I was worried this townhouse wouldn't be big enough, but it's almost as big as a house, with a fenced-in area out the sliding glass doors for a small backyard!* It is the first time I will be on my own with Luca since Graham my husband died, and I am equal parts exhilarated and scared to death. "Hey sis, where do you want this?" I hear my brother, Chandler, call out and I turn, seeing him come in the living room with the bedframe to Luca's bed.

"Let me show you his room," I reply to my brother as I go up the stairs. "I'm glad you and your friends were able to help me out today, and that Mom was okay with watching Luca. He would have been underfoot, and this way, I can get things mostly organized before he comes home later."

"Anything for you and you know that by now," Chandler says to me. "I know that things weren't great with you and Graham, and I'm proud of how you've managed to overcome all the shit that was slung your way when he died."

I shrug, there isn't anything I can do about it now, why let it consume my thoughts? Graham's parents hadn't liked me at all, feeling like I trapped their precious son into marriage by getting pregnant. Nothing could have been further from the truth. I had loved my husband, but he had treated me like a possession, something to be seen and not heard. It wasn't like that in the beginning, he truly loved me, but his parents' treatment towards me had influenced him the longer we had been married. My love for him had died long before he drew his last breath and the only reason I had stayed as long as I had was for Luca. "They were assholes, Chan, and hated me anyhow. They've made their position clear and I know that if Graham's will wasn't so airtight, they would have challenged it in court. At least, with the money he left, I don't have to work if I don't want to, you know?"

"Yeah, I hear you but knowing you, you'll find something because that's just how you are," he states. "Let me get little man's bed put together so we can set his room up and then we'll get yours set up."

"Works for me. How much is left in the truck?"

"Not much, we brought in all the boxes and put them where the labels said to put them, so other than setting up the beds and bringing in the dressers, you're all set."

This move has been easier than I thought it would be, if it wasn't for my brother and his friends this would've taken me days to complete on my own. This move was necessary, I needed to get myself and my son as far away from Graham's parents as possible, they are a force to be reckoned with and are determined to make my life a living hell.

Braxton

I step out into my backyard and fire up the grill. A soft voice from my left says, "Oh shit," and I hear the clatter of something dropping, then I hear a male voice ask, "What are you trying to do, sis? I told you I would bring that out."

"I know but you have your hands full and I thought I could handle it myself. Luca should be home soon, do you want to go ahead and order pizza? I'm sure he'll be hungry."

I feel bad eavesdropping on what appears to be my new neighbor, but then again, she *is* in her backyard so I figure it's fair game. There is something soothing about her tone that draws me to her and I shake my head. *You've obviously got a screw loose. She's a neighbor, nothing more, nothing less.* But hearing her voice does something to me, it is as if she is a siren calling out to me. *You're losing your damn mind Braxton,* I chastise myself.

Moving back into the house, I get the meat and then wrap the potatoes and set about putting them on the grill. I can hear her working and talking to herself as she puts together whatever it is that she'd initially dropped. I want to go and help her out, but feel she won't appreciate the intrusion. Just as I am rethinking my decision, I hear a little voice say, "Momma! I's home!"

"Hey, punkin, did you have fun with grandma?"

"Yeth! We played at the water slides and then? We went to her friend's house and made cookies!"

"Cookies, huh? How many did you eat?"

"Only a few, Momma," the little boy says, giggling. "What are you doing?"

"I'm putting together our firepit so we can sit out here and make s'mores."

"Can I help?" I can hear the eagerness in the little boy's voice.

"Absolutely. Hand me that thing over there, please."

"Momma? Do you think we can see if Daddy is watching us tonight?"

I gulp, sounds like the little guy is without a dad, just like my Lily has no mom. I hear the female voice say, "Come here, sweetie."

Several silent moments before I hear, "Look way up there, Luca, can you see that one?"

"Yeth! Is that Daddy?"

"I think so, yes, it's the brightest one in the sky. Bet he's peeking down to see how you like your

19

new room!" I can't help it, I find myself looking up, wondering which star she is referring to, I look for the brightest one I can find.

"I miss him, Momma." The sadness in the little boy's voice gets to me. *Poor guy.*

"I know, sweetie, I know."

"Momma? Will I ever have a daddy again?"

"I don't know sweetheart. Momma isn't dating anyone and in order for you to have that, I would have to date someone and then get married again."

"I hopes you finds someone Momma."

Definitely feeling as though I am intruding, I quickly finish grilling and take my meal inside. Good thing my daughter is fast asleep in her room, if she'd heard the little boy next door she'd want to go introduce herself and make a new friend. I'm too tired to venture over right now, *later* I think, I'll introduce myself and Lily later.

Later that night as I lay in bed my thoughts wander to my new neighbor. I can't help but feel sorry for her, knowing what it is like to be a single parent and how hard it is, I wonder if I shouldn't extend a lending hand. *It's hard for a man to raise a little girl, but I can't imagine a single woman trying to raise a boy. Boys need a man in their life, women have a hard time understanding the male mind...*that thought makes me laugh at myself, *as if women are any easier to understand.*

I drift off to sleep with thoughts of how I can help the lady next door.

Caraleigh

I lay in bed that night and can't get my thoughts off my son. *He's having such a rough time since his father's death.* Graham had ignored some symptoms he was having and ended up with Stage Four colon cancer. Major surgery had left him with a colostomy bag, but the damage was done. The cancer had metastasized and within two months, he was gone. I can only do so much for him, be so much to him. *He needs more, he needs a man to show him the way.* Sure, my brother is around and involved, but not the way Luca needs. Unless Chandler decides to move closer, his involvement will now be limited. He needs someone full time, someone who can help him grow and develop into the kind of man I pray he will become. *If only I could find that kind of man,* I can't help but think. Lord knows Graham didn't help when it comes to the way I view men. He became so cold, distant and neglectful and ignored me in every way a man can towards the end of our relationship. He never noticed if I was in the same room as him, he chose to ignore me more than talk to me. *He was such a good dad though, too bad that didn't extend to me,* are my last thoughts as I drift off to sleep.

I wake the next morning with a very excited little boy jumping on my bed. "I getsta go to a new school today Momma, hurry up and wakes up sleepyhead." I love his musings and the way he says certain words. He is the only joy I have left in my life, my failure as a wife still weighs on me deeply. I am determined to be the best mother to my little boy.

"Alright, alright, I'm up already," I say to him as I sit up in the bed and pull him into my lap for some cuddle time.

"Momma, no cuddles we havesta get ready," he says in his little boy excitement.

"Your clothes are laying in the living room on the couch, go get dressed while Momma does." He runs off in excitement. He loves making new friends, too bad I don't. I have friends, ones who will be here to visit soon, but making new ones isn't my cup of tea. I like *my* circle of friends, meeting new people always terrifies me, *never knowing who you can trust.*

After getting clothes on I go into the bathroom to brush my hair and teeth, looking into the mirror I can see how tired I look. *My looks definitely tell the tale of what life has been like for me lately.* Taking my eyes from the mirror, I pull my long hair into a ponytail and call it good enough. *Not like I have anyone to impress these days anyhow.* Coming out of my dark thoughts, I know I need to get this day going. *I need to feed Luca and get him to brush his teeth, a task that is easier said than done.* I decide to make him a big breakfast for his first day at a new school, pancakes and bacon—his favorite. I'd rather be able to give him something healthier, but today is a special occasion. Once he is done I know the tough part of the morning is just beginning.

"You need to brush your teeth now that you've eaten a good breakfast."

"But Momma..."

"Now young man." I give him my best stern mom look so he knows I'm not playing around with this.

"Okay Momma," he says to me as he hangs his head in defeat. Why he hates to brush his teeth so much is a mystery to me.

Once teeth are brushed and lunch is packed Luca and I run out the front door in a rush, his fear of being late for his first day is amusing.

"Lily, slow your britches," I hear coming from my left.

"Nan, we have to hurry or I'm gonna bees late," I hear a little girl respond. Looking around, I see an older woman with a beautiful little girl that she's finally caught up to. I smile and chuckle a little, it seems we are both suffering from over-excited children this morning.

The older woman, who the girl called Nan, grabs her hand and turns seeing me standing there smiling at them, with Luca's hand in mine.

"Good morning," she says to me.

"Morning, I see we both have excited children this morning," I say to her.

"My granddaughter loves school. Are you new around here dear?"

"Yes ma'am, we just moved in yesterday and today is Luca's first day."

"How exciting, this rambunctious little girl here is Lily."

"Hello Lily, this is my son Luca...say hello to Lily, Luca."

"Hi."

"Hey," she responds, "wanna comes plays with me after school today?"

"Yes! Can I Mom?"

"Sure you can, buddy, once homework is done if you have any."

"I can if I dossen't have any homework after school. If not I can play," he tells her like she didn't hear me when I responded to him.

"If you don't have homework," I correct him. He scowls at me unimpressed with my interference.

"That's what I said Momma!" Some days correcting his grammar just isn't worth the effort. He gets upset and offended, especially if I do it in front of other people.

"You're right, it has the same meaning." Man, being an adult and a parent isn't always fun. I hate adulting!

I walk up to Nan, saying, "I'm sorry I didn't introduce myself, I'm Caraleigh Jensen."

"You can call me Nan, dear, everyone does except for my son Braxton and his friends. They all call me Mom, all of his friends have since he was a young boy."

"Well, I better get this guy off to school, it was nice meeting you Nan and Lily. Come on Luca, let's get you to school." I turn and wave at Nan who is still standing in the same spot watching me. Once I'm in the car I notice her moving towards her own vehicle. *I wonder why she was just standing there staring at me?*

CHAPTER TWO

Braxton

I am so exhausted I barely noticed my little girl climb into my bed this morning and place a kiss on my cheek. That little girl is my world, and I can't imagine what my life without her would be like. When her mother took off and I was left alone trying to figure out how to raise my little girl, I was scared. I'm so thankful that my mother stepped in and taught me the things I needed to know.

The basics—how to bathe her, do her hair, change her diapers, fix her bottle, all of the everyday needs—wouldn't have gotten done without her help. She taught me the right way to do these things. *Too bad I didn't know about Youtube back then, sure would've come in handy.*

Climbing out of bed I go about getting ready for the day. After taking care of the necessities, shower, shave, toilet and brushing my teeth, I then go to my closet to get dressed. I hear my mother come in the house. "I'll be out in a minute, Mom," I yell out to her, wanting to know how the morning went with Lily.

Walking into the living room I can hear my mom in the kitchen, sounds like she's making breakfast. "Good morning, how did things go with Lily? Did she give you a hard time?"

"Not at all, she even made a new friend before we left the parking lot," Mom tells me.

Raising my eyebrows I wait for her to tell me more about this new friend. When she doesn't right away I ask curiously, "New friend, and who might that be, Mom?"

"There is a woman who moved in yesterday, she has a little boy that looks to be around Lily's age."

"And they what, struck up a conversation in the middle of the lot?" I ask, not liking that my little girl doesn't understand stranger danger.

"No dear, they were both excited to get to school and his mother and I commiserated on it and struck up a conversation. In turn the kids were introduced and set up a playdate for after school today."

"That's nice, his first day and he's already going with a friend. What time is this playdate?"

"We didn't set up an exact time, she wanted to make sure if he had homework that it was done before the kids met up to play."

I don't know why, but the thought of Lily having someone to play with at home, a little boy, terrifies me just a little. *I don't know if I'm ready for her to have a boy as a friend,* I can't help but think to myself.

Caraleigh

Needing to have something to do that day and keep my mind occupied, I get busy unpacking boxes that didn't get finished the day before. I start off in the kitchen, and by the time I need to leave to pick Luca up from school, I've made it through the living room boxes and have them broken down. *Two rooms down, four to go,* I think to myself. *Maybe while Luca is playing with Lily I can tackle his room and get it done before he makes it home. Sure would be a lot easier to do without him under my feet.*

With a game plan in mind, I grab my keys and purse and head out the door. The line to pick up Luca at the school is long and unorganized in my personal opinion. Kids are running around everywhere making me nervous. *They need to be keeping a better eye on these kids. One day one of these kids is going to be hurt or kidnapped.* Just the thought makes me sick to my stomach. Looks like something I should bring up at the next parent-teacher association meeting, hopefully they'll listen to me and take my fears seriously. *These kids are vulnerable and need more supervision than they have right now, they have no concept of danger at their ages.*

Finally I make my way up the line and spot Luca in the crowd of children. He is standing next to Lily and they have their heads together. *Uh-oh, those two are going to be trouble.* Rolling down the window I call out his name, his head pops up and a huge smile graces his face. I'll never get tired of seeing that look, I can be having the worst day and he'll grin at me and all my troubles will melt away. I wave at Lily and she waves back, I notice she has spotted her ride home as well. Now I won't feel bad about leaving Lily there by herself, I see my boy running to the car, papers in hand and excitement showing all over him.

"Did you have a good first day buddy?"

"It was the bestest, Momma! I gots to play with Lily at recess and we even have PE together."

"That's wonderful, Luca. Is Lily in your grade?"

"Nah, she's in kindergarten and I'm in first." Like I can ever forget my baby is no more, he's a young man now. When he was in kindergarten I could still get away with thinking of him as my baby, but that is a thing of the past. He feels older and braver since he passed to the next level of school, and I take on his mentality. I never want to make him feel less than what he is feeling, I want him to grow up learning to think on his own and able to solve his own problems. I'll be right there beside him, helping him along the way, helping him out in any way he'll allow me to.

"I's don't have any homeworks today. Can I go right over to Lily's and play?"

"Let's make sure that her Nan doesn't have anything she needs to do first." I can see him in the corner of my eye as he crosses his arms and pouts. He doesn't possess much patience, but then again, I don't know any kid his age that does. "I promise, buddy, you'll get to play with Lily, now turn that frown upside down." I can see his face light up as he giggles at what I said.

"You're so silly Momma."

"What?" I feign being shocked. "You couldn't mean me?" I gasp out causing him to laugh harder. These interactions between us are the highlight of my day. *If it wasn't for him, I'd be a sad, bitter pile of misery lying on the floor.*

Once at home, I get him into the house and help him unload his backpack. I feel it is important that he learns early on to do certain things for himself. As I am looking through the papers he has brought home with him, he empties out his lunchbox and puts it on the counter. "Go get changed into play clothes, Luca, while I get these papers signed, okay?"

"Okay, Momma. Can I have a snack?"

"I'll have one ready for you when you get back downstairs, okay?"

"Yeth!" he exclaims, already running up the stairs. I smile as I sort his papers into things I need to read, sign and return, and the things he has done today. Looking in his backpack, I see a folder with his name on it, along with a weekly agenda. Reading over it, I see that the only homework he has is to read for twenty minutes. Since we read every night before bed, I go ahead and sign off for today's reading time. Going to the fridge, I pull out the plate of fruit I put together for him before I left to pick him up. Then I get him a glass of ice water to go with his after-school snack. With everything now on the table, I go back to reading and signing papers. *Jeez, how many times do they need my emergency contact information?* It isn't like I have a lot of options to add along with mine, with Graham dead and his family not involved, and mine too far away, it's only me. I hear him as he comes running back down the stairs and hide my smile as he skids into the kitchen, plopping down in his seat.

"Luca?" I ask.

"Yeth Momma?" he replies, already eating a strawberry.

"Remember we don't run up and down the stairs. You could fall and hurt yourself."

He sighs. He doesn't like forgetting the rules and always feels bad when he does. "I'm sorry, Momma. I forgot."

"I know you did and I also know how excited you are to go play with Lily, I just wanted to remind you, okay? Since that's kind of my job as your mom," I tell him, putting the signed papers into the

31

folder then getting up and putting it into his backpack so he'll have it for tomorrow.

Once he finishes his snack, I help him take care of his dishes. There's no way I want any child of mine unable to take care of themselves! "Okay, little man, go wash your hands and we'll walk next door and see if Lily can play now," I tell him. When he goes running out of the room, I laugh and then sigh. I guess he forgot "Rule Number One—No Running" again.

"I'm ready, Momma," he says as he runs back into the kitchen. Seeing my look, he drops his head and says, "I forgotted again, didn't I?"

"You did, but that's why I'm the momma. I'll keep reminding you until you remember, okay? You ready to go next door?"

He grabs my hand and starts pulling me toward the front door and I have to laugh at his excitement.

"Slow down little man, there's no rush, Lily isn't going anywhere." I laugh at his exuberance and am excited for him and his new friendship.

At the house next door, I knock as Luca jumps up and down. When a man opens the door, my words fail me. He's big, one of the tallest men I've ever seen and he's definitely not a suit kind of wearing man. No, not the way those muscles stretch the t-shirt he has on over a pair of jeans that are molded to him like a second skin. "Can I help you?" he asks. Hearing that deep baritone sends shivers through me and catches me off guard. I've never reacted to anyone like I am to him and have only been in his presence for a matter of minutes, if that!

"Uh, hi, I'm your new neighbor. We met Nan and Lily this morning and set up a playdate for the two kids," I manage to stammer.

He looks me up and down and I can feel every inch of it as he visually examines my body. I feel a shiver run through me and am taken off guard with the way I'm reacting as he looks at me the way I perused him only moments ago. I feel like I can't get words to leave my mouth, I only want to stand here and continue admiring the view in front of me. I am brought out of these thoughts when Luca tugs on my hand.

"Momma, can I plays with Lily now?" I see this man who's taken my rational thoughts look away from me and down at my son.

"Hello Luca, my name is Braxton and I'm Lily's dad, she's been waiting for you to come play with her. She's in the backyard, would you like to go join her?"

"Yes!" Luca screams out while jumping up and down. Still having a hold of my hand, I feel my body jerking with his exuberance. "I'm gonnas go play with Lily now Momma, love you," he says to me as he lets go of my hand and takes off in their house heading towards the back door.

I yell out, "Be good Luca, I'll be here in two hours to pick you up."

"Yes ma'am," he hollers back never stopping long enough to look at me. Standing here in front of any woman's wet dream, I try to make my mouth work so I can tell him I'll be back and thank him for allowing Luca to come to his house and play.

"Umm...thank you for allowing Luca over to play with Lily this afternoon. I'll be back at five to pick him up," I stammer out as I turn around to walk away. I don't make it far before I feel a hand on my wrist stopping my hasty retreat.

"Won't you come in and have something to drink before you take off? I'd like to get to know my neighbor and my daughter's newest friend's mom." Yes, I want that very much, I think to myself but wonder if it's a wise decision to make. It's been a long time since a man has affected me this much with his presence alone...hell who am I kidding, it's never happened. That alone scares the everloving crap out of me.

"Sure," I say, "but I can't stay long, I still have some unpacking I need to get done while Luca is busy and not under my feet the entire time. Entertaining a little boy while trying to get the house organized is harder than you'd think," I giggle, unsure of what to do or say. Dammit, I'm making a fool of myself and I feel my cheeks heat with embarrassment.

He must think I'm a complete idiot since I can't seem to get my thoughts straight. Of course he knows what it's like to have a kid underfoot, I bet he's now looking forward to me walking out his door and go home.

"What would you like to drink?" he asks me, maybe I haven't completely screwed this up.

"Water will be fine, thank you."

"I have beer and wine if you'd like to kick back and relax some."

"I don't usually drink until Luca is in bed for the night, maybe some other time," I say hoping he'll want to do this again another day without the kids here.

"So tell me, what brings you to our town?"

"I needed to get away from my deceased husband's family, this place is far enough away from them that I feel comfortable and it's a good place for me and Luca to start over again."

"Your husband passed away, I'm sorry to hear that." And I can tell by the way he says it that he's sincere in what he said.

"We were married, but we didn't love or respect each other anymore." Why in the hell am I telling him any of this? I must be losing my mind while consumed by his good looks and southern charm. I need to get out of here as soon as it's been an acceptable amount of time!

He gets up and goes to get my water and him a beer, he comes back with a bottle of water and a bottle of beer. I can't help but admire the way he moves, he has a manly grace about the way he walks and holds his body. A body I really want to admire without that shirt on. I want to see his chest and count his abs that I can tell through that tight shirt that he has, but I can't tell to what extent that is.

"So do you work?" he asks me.

"I haven't since Luca was born, but now that it's just us, I plan to find something," I tell him as I open my bottle of water. Taking a sip, I mentally think *even though I don't have to work, I can't stare at four walls all day long.*

"Well, you'll find out soon enough since you'll hear my bike, but I belong to the new MC in town and we're in the process of opening up several businesses."

MC? What the hell is that? "I... I don't know what that means," I say feeling embarrassed.

"Motorcycle club," he replies before turning his bottle up and taking a long drink. Watching the way his throat moves has my brain synapses misfiring and I feel like drool may be pooling around my lips. Seeing the look on my face, he further clarifies, "My club isn't into illegal shit. All of our businesses are legitimate. We just like the freedom to do as we please, but for the most part, we're like your everyday average working man."

Yeah, right, like any of the working men I've ever seen look like him! "So I'll probably hear motorcycles?" I question.

36

"There's no probably about it, but if I'm coming home late from a trip, I will bring my cab, not my bike home."

"Your cab?" he must think I'm pretty naive since I haven't a clue what a cab is.

"The cab to my eighteen-wheeler, the front of the truck without the trailer part," he tells me with a smirk on his face.

Needing to change the subject so I'm not looking at his smile and how it transforms his face I ask, "Is that what that big building is on the other side?"

"Yeah, we built that so that I could pull the cab in and keep it secure. We only have a few trucks so far and while crime isn't big in this town, why take chances? Plus, it's big enough for my pickup truck when the weather turns too wet to ride."

"That makes sense." I want to know so much, like what happened to Lily's mom and is he seeing anyone, but I quickly realize that there's no way that I'll be asking those questions any time soon. Finished with my water, I stand and say, "Thank you for the drink, but I better see if I can get his room unpacked before he's done playing."

He stands as well and replies, "I can throw something on the grill, why don't you come back around six thirty and it'll be done by then. That'll give you a little more time to unpack, won't it?"

Shit as tongue-tied as I've been this past twenty or so minutes, now he wants me to eat dinner with

37

them? Out loud I say, "I'd like that, thank you. He tries hard to help, but I'm sure you know that a child's help usually means more work."

He chuckles as he follows me to the door. "Yeah, they try their best though and that's all we can really ask, isn't it?"

"You're right. Okay, I'll come back around six thirty then. Do you want me to bring anything?"

"Just yourself."

"I can do that, if Luca is any trouble just bring him home, thank you again for the drink." I say as I stand and practically run to the front door. *I'm acting like a teenager—hormones and all.*

CHAPTER THREE

Braxton

I walk her to the door, admiring the way her trim yet curvy body moves in a pair of leggings. She's got curves for days and I feel my hands clenching to keep from pulling her toward me. I've never had this kind of reaction to any woman, not even Lily's mom. "See you after while," I say, as I hold the door for her.

"See you then," she replies, her eyes not quite meeting mine. She's a shy little thing, but I think it may have more to do with the stuff she blurted out while we were talking than her true personality. Remembering how she and her brother talked in the backyard, I'm convinced I'm right. Once she walks out the door I have to adjust myself, she does things to me that I haven't experienced in many years. I need to think of anything to get my mind off the raging hard on I'm now sporting, then it's like an ice cold bucket of water rains down upon me as I hear Lily and Luca's voices outside.

I head back out to the yard and see my mom sitting in a chair while Lily and Luca play. "Mom? Going to run and pick up some chicken and stuff to throw on the grill, want me to grab a couple of salads?"

My mom looks at me with a knowing look before saying, "I take it we're having dinner guests?"

"We are, I told Caraleigh to come back around six thirty for dinner. That will give her a little more time to unpack."

"You're a good man, Braxton."

"Raised by a good mom," I reply.

At the store, I grab a buggy and head toward the meat department. I've got enough time to marinade the chicken the way I like it, which I prefer. The pre-packaged meats are okay, but when I have the time, I like to add my own seasonings.

"Hi, Braxton," a voice calls out. Turning I see one of the women who work in the office at the trucking company. Mentally steeling myself, I turn to face her.

"Hello, Starla," I respond. I haven't missed her blatant interest toward me but I don't shit where I eat so that's not gonna happen. Besides, she's not exactly my type. She has dieted to within an inch of her life and has bleach blonde hair. Not that I'm against a woman coloring her hair because I'm not, but when it looks like straw? Yeah, not so attractive.

"Oh, you're cooking out?" she asks, eyeing my cart.

"Yep. Just ran down to pick a few things up so I can get dinner started."

"Wow, a man who cooks," she replies. Cue the eye fucking that she's now giving me. While I want to shudder in distaste, my mom raised me to be a gentleman. I may be the president of an MC, but I won't treat a woman like shit unless all other means have been exhausted.

"Mostly grilling, but yeah, my mom taught me to cook."

"I love chicken on the grill."

"We do as well," I tell her, deliberately missing her hint. "Hate to cut this short, but I have a few more things to grab before I head out. See you tomorrow." There, that should shut her down.

"Uh...okay. Enjoy your evening."

"You do the same, Starla."

Finishing up with my purchases I head out of the grocery store, anxious to make it home.

Walking in the front door I hear Lily calling out for me, knowing that she heard me pull up I wonder how long she's been waiting for me to make it home. "Coming Lily," I say as I make my way towards the back yard. Once I step through the back door I can't help but laugh at the predicament Luca finds himself in. "What'cha doing up in the tree like a cat, Luca?"

"Lily threw the ball up in the air, Mr. Braxton and I was climbing up here to get it down for her, onlys I can't get myself down."

"Cans you helps him, Daddy?" my little girl asks as she looks up at me beneath her lashes. When she gives me that look I'd do anything in the world for her.

"Of course I will, baby girl, we can't leave him up in that tree like a stray kitten, now, can we?" They both giggle their childlike laughter at me, and it soothes something in my soul. I don't know how, but in just this moment alone this boy has dug his claws in me and I vow to always be there for him, regardless of what may or may not transpire between his mother and myself. I reach up on my toes and extend my arms for him to fall into. Once he decides he can trust me to catch him he lets go and lands in my arms. I give his hair a tussle and kiss him on top of his head. *He's a good boy, his mom's done a fine job with him.*

"Thank yous, Mr. Braxton, I was getting lonely and scared up in that tree alls by myselfs," he says gracing me with a smile that I'm committing to memory, I want to see his face light up like this on a daily basis...*woah,* where did that thought come from? Deciding to not think about it I let it go for now and will ponder this later.

"I need to get dinner going, Luca. You and your mom are going to eat with us, how does grilled chicken, salad, corn on the cob and green beans sound to you two?"

"Yes."

"Oh yeah."

I laugh at their exuberance, I guess what I have planned to cook for dinner sounds like a winner to them. Letting them get back to their playtime, I head into the house to get the charcoal so I can get the grill started so it has time to heat up and cook the chicken to perfection. Once I have the grill going, I start marinating the chicken, my marinade is inserted so I don't need to do it overnight. I grab the corn from the pantry and shuck it, once that's done I wrap it in tin foil coated in butter and seasoning. About this time mom walks in to help me prep dinner, I try to cook when I'm home giving my mother a break.

Mom eyes me as I'm getting things gathered for the grill. I see a glint in her eye and know what she's thinking.

"Don't go playing matchmaker, Mom, this will play out how it's meant to be. Let it alone and put your sights on one of the guys, I have Lily, they have no one other than the club."

"I don't know what you're talking about, Son, I don't interfere in your relationships," she says sounding innocent. Ha! I know she's anything but.

"Sure you don't. Mom, remember the lady at the grocery store and how you had a feeling she'd be a great mother and wife? You wanted me to go to the checkout line and ask her out, when I refused you set up a blind date behind my back?"

"She was a sweet woman who was lonely like you were, I had a feeling she could make you and

Lily happy, sweetheart, if you'd have given her a chance things might have happened."

"Mom, are you serious? She's fifty-four years old, a little old for me don't you think?"

"What? It isn't like she'd be a cougar or anything, Son, she's only twenty or so years older than you, she has experience with life and would have made your life easier. I just want to see you happy, is that so wrong? A mother likes to see her child not struggle to raise his child and likes to see a smile upon his face."

"I understand that, Mom, I really do, but let me find that person that will make me happy. I want that feeling, the one that slams into you out of nowhere, that one person that you can't breathe without. I want my heart to jump with excitement when I look at her face. It will happen, Mom, just maybe not on your timeline. I know you want me happy, I want me happy, I want Lily to have a woman to look up to, to teach her about makeup, talk boys with her," I cringe at that thought. "Most of all, I want to know that neither she or I will be abandoned again, I need that security. I'd like to think I'll know that person when I meet her, give me a chance before you doom me to a lifetime of loneliness and misery." Mom wipes a tear from under her eye, which makes my heart break. I can't stand to see a woman cry, but especially not my Mom.

"Don't cry, Mom, I promise I'm still enjoying life with Lily and you. You two make my life worth waking up every morning and coming home every night. You two are all I need for now," but I can't help but imagine having Caraleigh and Luca added to those days and nights.

"You make your mom a very happy woman, you've grown into a man I'm proud to call mine." I bring Mom into a hug showing her what her love and life commitment means to me.

At six o'clock I throw the chicken and corn on the grill. The salad is made and sitting in the fridge and Mom is working on the green beans and getting the outside table set. It's been such a nice day that I figure eating outside will be a fun treat for the kids. I set out the citrus candles to keep the bugs and mosquitos away. I'm keeping an eye on the kids and their laughter is music to my ears. Seeing Lily be so carefree and enjoying life is something I'll never tire of watching. Luca is fitting in with our family as if he's always been meant to be a part of us.

"Hey kids, why don't y'all go get yourselves washed up for dinner and we'll bring out the bubbles to play with until dinner is done."

"Okays, Daddy," Lily says as she grabs Luca's hand and pulls on it, giving him a silent command to follow her. Even at her age, she's figured out how to get boys to do her bidding. Wow, women start young and I never realized how young until just this moment.

"Yes, sirs, will my momma be here soon?" Luca asks as he digs in his feet for some resistance while waiting on my answer.

"Ya, buddy, she'll be here any minute."

They take off in the house and I hear my mom laughing at them. "She already has him wrapped around her finger," she says as she walks past me into the house. *She has him wrapped around her finger and he's already protective of her*, I think to myself, *her having a boy for a friend might come in handy later on down the road.*

"He better be the only boy," I mutter under my breath. I don't like my baby girl liking boys...period, friendship and all.

"What was that, Son?" Mom asks coming up behind me, scaring the absolute shit out of me, I nearly scream out like a little bitch.

"Mom! Since when did you become a ninja? Coming up behind me all stealth-like and shit, are you trying to give me a heart attack woman?"

Mom starts laughing at me, and we're not talking a cute little woman's laugh either, she's bent over holding her stomach with tears streaming out of her eyes. I'm glad she finds this shit funny, I'm the motherfucking president of an MC, it shouldn't be so easy to sneak up behind me!

"Oh, Braxton. Son, you make an old woman laugh like this. I wasn't being quiet in the least, as a matter of fact I dropped the platter of appetizers on the table and it scared me to death. How it is you didn't hear me doing that is beyond me, Son," she says while still laughing as she's speaking to me. "You were just so lost in your thoughts anyone and anything around you was just background noise. You really should be more aware of your surroundings, Son."

"Ha-ha, very funny, woman! I swear you took ten years off of my life just now," I say pouting. Yes, I know grown men don't pout, but Mom still has the ability to make me act like a child.

Just as she goes to retort we hear a scream and a door slam, and my heart drops. I know that's Caraleigh, don't ask me how I know I just know that's my woman's scream. *My woman,* what the fuck has gotten into me? She's turning me into a fucking teenager. As I go to run through the house and out my front door I see a head poke up over the fence line that separates my house from hers.

"Um, Braxton?"

"What the hell, woman? Between you and my mom I'm going to have grey hair before my time, what's up with all that screaming and door slamming?"

"Well, I was going out my door to come to your house, but see...there's this huge beast that started growling at me and charging at my door. It scared

47

the absolute shit out of me, think you could help me out here?"

"A dog? Seriously! There aren't any dogs allowed on the premises, there's kids and elderly folks living here. It states in the contract no large dogs of any kind are allowed," I say, fuming out loud.

"That's all good and dandy, but doesn't help my situation at all, Braxton. Could you get rid of the dog please?"

"Let me get this straight, you want me to go out and confront an attack dog?"

"Um, yes?" she says, but it's more question-like than a statement.

"I don't think so woman! I like my balls where they are, attached to me and not in a dog's mouth!" And I'm completely serious, my friend was attacked when we were children and the damn dog went right after his nuts. Ain't no way in hell that will be happening to me. No way, no how.

"Then what are you going to do about it?"

"I'm calling animal control, hang on and hold tight and I'll get back to you." I grab my phone and call, they say it will be at least an hour before they have a handler here that can come and get the beast. They are a no-kill shelter which works for me, I can't fathom the thought of any animal being put down unless there is absolutely no choice in the matter. Even then it pisses me off that an animal was put in that position by an animal's owner. They are like children, they depend on you for shelter, food and love. If they aren't given those they can become rabid and unsavable. If that happens I'd personally like to go a few rounds with said owner.

"It's going to be at least an hour, sweetheart."

"So what are we going to do? Are you going to hand me my son over the fence along with my dinner?"

"Hell no, I have two ladders, we'll put one on your side and one on mine and you can climb over that way. Once we're done eating the animal should be gone and getting medical attention." I've been looking forward to this night, no way am I not going to spend it with her. Nothing is getting in my way.

"Alright, Braxton, sounds good to me," she tells me. Now that that's settled I grab my mom to watch the grill while I get my ladders. Just the thought of watching her ass move while she climbs down on my side has me adjusting myself for what feels like the hundredth time today and brings yet another smile to my face.

Caraleigh

As I get the ladder situated on my side I climb up and notice he has the other ladder ready for me. I

49

straddle the fence, put my foot out for the ladder, and I feel his hand touch me to guide me over. Chills run through my body, what is this guy doing to me? I can't help where my mind wanders to, feeling those hands run up and down my body caressing me in ways that haven't been done in many years. Then I hear, "Sure you're alright, sweetheart?"

I come away from my delicious thoughts and tell him, "I'm fine, just a little nervous to miss my step," and I carry on. Once I have both feet planted on the ladder I feel his hands grab my waist and nearly moan out loud at the contact.

The tingles that race down my spine are something new, something I've never felt before. I hope I get to experience his hands on me many times over. Firmly planted on the ground I turn around and come face to face with the man I've been daydreaming about ever since he opened his door and invited me in.

"Thank you for helping me, I'm clumsy sometimes and was worried I'd fall flat on my butt." The thought of falling and landing on my backside has embarrassed me even though it didn't actually happen. I didn't lie when I said I'm clumsy, my family doesn't let me climb anything that I could potentially fall from. My brother especially freaks out when I try to take on jobs that entail me having to reach, climb or stand on any objects.

"No problem, sweetheart, and just so you know as long as I'm around to catch you, you'll never fall on my watch," he says as he winks at me causing a blush to cover my body. *I can't wait to find out what else he can do to my body.* Those thoughts go away quickly when I hear my little guy call out for me.

"Momma, you're here!"

"I am, buddy, have you been having fun with Lily?"

"The bestest time! I'm so glad we moved here Momma, Lily is my new bestest friend."

"Oh yeah? I don't think we should tell that to Ralynn...it may hurt her feelings," I tell him, Ralynn is my best friend's daughter, she and Luca have grown up together and have always been inseparable.

"It wonts hurt her feelins, Momma, yous silly. Ralynn's my bestest friend there and Lily is here. Theys still both my bestest."

"Well, that's good to hear because she and Donna Jo are coming to visit next week!"

"Yay! Lily yous gonna like Ralynn, she is so much fun," he says dragging out the so as dramatically as he can.

"Did you hears that, Daddy? I get to makes another friend."

"That's great, baby girl," Braxton tells her, "one can't have too many friends." He winks at her causing both kids to laugh and I can't help the

51

chuckle that escapes my mouth along with them. He's such a good dad, it makes me miss Graham, not for me, but for Luca. He needs a dad in his life, and I feel guilty that he no longer has one.

"Momma, Lily is gonna helps me look up in the sky for Daddy tonight. We're gonna tell him that we're bestest friends."

"You are huh?" I can't stop the tears as they gather in my eyes. I turn my back and bend over pretending my shoe needs to be tied so he doesn't see his momma holding back her tears.

"Her momma's gone too, but she's not up in the sky like my dad is. So we don't have to tell her about us, Lily says she just left her. Why would a momma leave her kid?" Leave it to kids to ask the tough questions. I look at Braxton and see his head hanging down, I don't know if it's because he misses Lily's mom or if he's unsure of how to answer Luca's question.

Braxton bends down in front of the kids and takes Lily's hands in his. "Sometimes, adults can't handle the responsibility of having kids. Lily's mom couldn't, so she left her with me to love and take care of."

"What's responbility?" Luca asks Braxton.

"Responsibility," I correct him which causes him to roll his eyes at me.

"May I?" I ask Braxton before I jump in.

"By all means, please."

"When a parent has a child, not only do they love them, but they are responsible for taking care of all of their needs. Like when I help you with homework, taking a bath, cleaning your room and making you something to eat. It means I am responsible for making sure all of your needs are taken care of, that you never have to do it all by yourself. Just like your goldfish you had, you were responsible for feeding him, cleaning his water and talking to him so he didn't get lonely."

"Yes! I was responbible."

"Yes you were, I love you," I tell him, needing to let him know in my way how proud I am of him, and very thankful this conversation is coming to a close.

He and Lily run off and start blowing bubbles, it brings back a lot of memories from my childhood. My brother and I used to love to blow bubbles and run around the yard popping them. I watch as the kids do the same and start laughing at how much fun they're having. I'm so happy that Luca has made a friend he can play with here at home. While watching them I'm also keeping an eye on Braxton and Nan as they finish up on the grill.

"Anything I can do to help?" I ask, feeling like a freeloader just sitting here.

"You're our guest sweetheart, just sit back and relax," Nan tells me. "I made some sweet tea earlier, would you like a glass, dear?"

"That sounds amazing, I would love a glass, Nan."

"Were you able to get a lot of unpacking accomplished?" Braxton sits next to me and asks.

"I did actually, Luca's room is finished and so is the guest bathroom. It doesn't seem like a lot, but to me it will make life easier. Luca will have all of his toys to keep him occupied so that I can finish my room and bathroom. You don't realize how much stuff you have until it's time to pack it up and then put it away."

"I remember, it wasn't that long ago that Mom, Lily and I moved here. We were the first tenants and Lily was bored out of her mind. We made sure her room was settled before any of the other rooms were even touched. I was never so grateful in my life to say goodbye to fast food as I was when the kitchen was finally done."

"I did it opposite, Luca and I only have fast food on rare occasions. I like him to have as much healthy food as possible. Too much sugar and sodium makes for a very miserable time for mom."

"He gets hyperactive, huh?"

"That he does, he already is like a locomotive on a good day, I'm constantly sitting and wondering when the caboose will show itself." I laugh at my own analogy of my son and his active lifestyle and he joins me in the laughter. "What about Lily?"

"That girl of mine can sit and play by herself for hours. She's always been able to entertain herself with her dolls and kitchen playset. I sometimes have to go in search of her just to check and make sure she's alright. She'll be so quiet I'll start to wonder to myself if she's taken off on me. I think the quietness is more nerve wracking than when she's being loud and rambunctious."

"I think if I was to go without hearing Luca for any amount of time I'd freak out. He hasn't been quiet since the day he was born. He's always been so curious, and ever since he started walking he's been into anything and everything his hands can get ahold of. It would drive me crazy wondering if the house was baby-proofed well enough."

"I know! Lily was a really good baby, but when she started pulling herself up on furniture and grabbing anything in sight I started bubble wrapping things up. Mom used to laugh at me and tell me I was being melodramatic, but all I could see was her hurting herself. Scared the life out of me on most days."

"I know what you mean, I used to spend my days following him around for fear of what he'd find next." I am enjoying hearing the way he talks about Lily, you can see the love pouring from his eyes as he talks about her. I want that for Luca.

"So earlier you mentioned that a friend of yours was coming for a visit? When do you expect her here?"

"She'll be here with her daughter Ralynn in four days," I say excitedly, she's my closest friend since childhood and I can't wait to see her. I know it's only been a few days, but I already miss her terribly.

"What about Ralynn's school, won't she miss too many days?"

"No, she homeschools Ralynn...the school she'd have to attend isn't the best. Donna Jo can't afford to send her to a private school so she chooses to work from home that way she can keep her daughter safe and play teacher at the same time."

"I would do the same thing if it meant keeping Lily safe," he tells me.

"I agree, I helped her find the right homeschool program and it's worked out well for Ralynn. She's a very smart little girl and hasn't had a hard time adjusting to it. She picks things up quickly and I swear she could probably jump a grade or two if Donna Jo wanted to explore it further. She won't though, because she eventually wants Ralynn back in the public school system. She wants her to have socialization skills and to make friends. She's looking to move and I'm hoping to talk her into moving here with me."

"Sounds like it would be a good move for her and Ralynn. You say she works from home? What does she do?" I don't tell many people what Donna Jo does for a living, some like to judge her, but I have a feeling he won't.

"Promise not to judge her?"

"I'd never judge someone on what they have to do for a living to support themselves and their child," he states matter-of-factly.

"She writes adult romance books."

"So what you're trying to tell me is she writes those books for women with sex in them?"

"Yep," I tell him waiting for his reaction.

"That's awesome, Mom likes to read those types of books. Maybe you can tell her about your friend so she can pick up one of hers to read."

"I'll do one better, she usually has some on hand and I'll have her bring one for your mom when she comes."

"Really? Let her know I'll pay her for a copy, I know that shit's not free," he says.

"Nope, not this first one, at least," I tell him. He shakes his head at me and grins before looking over his shoulder at the kids.

"I'm glad they're getting along so well."

"Me too," I reply. "Luca hasn't had too many friends because when his dad got sick, we had to watch who came around."

"That had to be hard on y'all."

"It was...challenging. I hated it for Luca because despite everything, his dad loved him and doted on him."

"What about you?" he asks me.

"What do you mean?"

"Well, how was it challenging?" *Ugh, he asks the tough questions.*

57

I sigh before saying, "His parents never liked me and after some time, he adopted their behaviors toward me. When he got sick, his mom was around all the time and I did even less right than before. The tension was so high you could have cut it with a knife and I got to where all I focused on was making sure Luca wasn't impacted."

He reaches over and squeezes my hand and replies, "That couldn't have been easy on you at all."

"It wasn't, but I focused on him and powered through. And now we're here, ready for new beginnings."

Picking up his beer, he clinks it against my glass of sweet tea and says, "To new beginnings."

CHAPTER FOUR

Braxton

Dinner has finally been served and we're all listening to the kids tell us all about their playdate today and how much fun they've had.

"Can we do this every day, Daddy?" my beautiful little girl asks me.

"I'm not sure about every day, baby girl, but we can make sure y'all get together a couple of times a week. Luca and you will have homework and they have friends coming for a visit in a couple of days. We don't want to intrude on that," I tell her, hoping to appease her some.

"Lily would never be an intrusion to us, Braxton," Caraleigh tells me and I can't help but focus my eyes on her lips as she talks. Lips I can't help but imagining doing all kinds of dirty things to my body. I snap my eyes up to meet hers.

"Anytime you feel like having her over just let me know and either Mom or I'll bring her on over."

"I was thinking of taking Luca to the playground near the school when they get out tomorrow, would it be alright for me to pick Lily up from the school and take her with us? We won't be long, maybe an hour, two tops."

"Pease Daddy, pease can I go?"

"As long as you promise to do your homework as soon as you get home without complaining."

"I pwomise, Daddy, I'll be good and not compain any."

"Complain, baby girl, not compain, and I'll call the school tomorrow and give permission for Caraleigh to pick you up."

"Yay," Luca and Lily both shout and do little shimmies in their chairs. They're acting like they didn't just spend the entire afternoon and evening together.

"Sounds like a plan to me, let me help you guys clean up this mess and then Luca and I need to head home. He needs a bath and I need to snuggle in my bed with an e-reader and a glass of wine. It's been a long day," Caraleigh says to us.

"Nonsense, you two get the kids bathed and in bed and I'll handle the clean up tonight," Mom says.

"Are you sure, Mom? I don't mind helping."

"Like I said, take care of the kids, I've got this. Why don't you and Lily walk Caraleigh and Luca home, Braxton," Mom says, she has that look in her eyes again, I have a feeling the matchmaking has begun. I sigh knowing our conversation from before has long been forgotten.

"Alright, Mom, if you insist." I give her a smirk letting her know I'm on to her game. "Come on, Lily, let's walk our friends home."

"You don't have to do that, Braxton, we're just next door," Caraleigh says to me.

"No, we don't mind, do we, Lily?"

"Nah Daddy, we don't mind," she says grabbing Luca's hand causing my heart to temporarily combust. In my mind her holding his hand is innocent, but my heart can't take it. That's my baby girl and she shouldn't be holding any boy's hand, only mine. Period, end of story. I look over at Caraleigh to get her reaction, only she has a big smile on her face, I can tell I'm all alone in this situation.

"They're holding hands," I tell her as if it isn't obvious.

"I know, isn't it sweet?" she says to me and I mentally roll my eyes at her. Sweet, yeah it's giving me a sweet tooth alright. *Fuck!*

Suddenly I can't wait to get our guests to their house so I can take my baby girl's hand and hold it in my own. I'll make sure to scrub that hand extra well during her bath time. Mind made up, I grab Caraleigh's hand and practically run for the front door. Her laughter following in my wake, I say, "What? I know they both need baths, let's get this show on the road people."

Her laughter should be making me happy, instead it's making me anxious. What is wrong with these people? They're too young to be holding hands for Christ's sake. Now, feeling Caraleigh's soft, small hand in mine? Totally different story as I

61

intertwine our fingers, earning a look from her. Smiling, I squeeze her hand and lead us out the door.

Later that night I get a call that our run that we thought had been cancelled was renewed. Guess who's going out of town for the next couple of days...yep me. I'm bummed about this seeing as I was looking forward to crashing their playdate at the playground just to spend some time with Caraleigh. There is something about her that I can't quite put my finger on, she does something to me that I'm looking forward to exploring. Just looks like those plans are going to take a little longer than I'd first anticipated. A couple of days away shouldn't kill me...right?

A lesser man than me would let this get him down...for me, however, it just makes me get a game plan in place. I want to show her what I'm all about, introduce her to the guys. Sounds like we need to plan a BBQ, maybe as a welcome to town party. With a plan in mind I text my VP to have him set it up, now I need to get this run done and get back home.

Fuck, everything that could go wrong on this run has gone wrong. From the trailer not being refrigerated like it was supposed to, to the supplier not having their shit together when I arrived. Wishing I was anywhere but here, I listen to the foreman yelling at the dockworkers, as if it was their fault that he didn't get the correct trailer. Sighing, I head over to a forklift and climb up. Maybe if I give them a hand, I'll be out of here and headed to the delivery point sooner rather than later, right?

"And then we swang really high, Daddy!" she exclaims in my ear. Hearing about her playdate at the park has me all kinds of homesick, but I promised myself when I had to start making these trips that I would call Lily every night so I could hear about her day.

"Swung, sweetie. You swung really high. Did you like it?" I ask her. It's been ten minutes of non-stop chatter and while my heart smiles that she has a new friend, it also clenches at the thoughts that her friend is a boy. Then again, Luca seems to have a protective streak when it comes to her. I noticed that the other night walking them home. Since they live right next door, we actually took a little walk beforehand. He walked on the outside near the parking lot. Granted, they were still holding hands, but whatever. I'll work harder to delete the sight of her little hand enclosed in his. Maybe. Although...I did enjoy the feel of Caraleigh's hand in mine. Thinking of how soft her hand was, I mentally groan. I think I've jacked off more since meeting my delectable neighbor than I did when I first found out it felt good.

"I did! And guesses what? Miss Caraleigh taked us for *ice cream* when we got done playing! And I still ate all my dinner, too," she tells me.

"That sounds like a lot of fun, Lily. How's school?"

"It's good, Daddy. We is reading a new book about kitties!"

"You are?"

"Yes, they is silly kitties, too. They thinks there are vampires and ghosts!"

"Hmm, is Nan reading them to you?"

"No, Daddy, we is reading them in class. The teacher even has finger puppets!" she whispers, her voice so full of excitement it vibrates through the phone. I can picture her face—eyes wide, grin showing with those damn dimples that will likely cause me a heart attack when she hits her teen years.

"Well, I'll look and see if I can find you a copy when I get home, okay?" I ask her.

"*Really?*" she squeals, causing me to pull the phone away from my ear.

"Yes, really. Do you think Luca would like his own copy?"

"Prolly so, Daddy. Him is learning to read harder books like this one."

"Then I'll get him one too, how's that sound?"

"You're the bestest daddy ever!"

"Okay, pumpkin, let me talk to Nan, okay?"

"Bye, Daddy, love you!" she says before I hear Mom take the phone.

"When will you be back, Braxton?" she asks me after saying hello.

"Probably another day or so, Mom. I picked up another run on the way back from a customer."

"Will you be back in time for the barbeque?"

"Honestly? I'm not sure. And I don't want to miss it, but you know we're trying to get our name out there and build business and unfortunately, the buck stops here."

"You work too hard, Son."

"Mom, we've been over this - until we get a few more of the businesses up and running, it is what it is. How is Caraleigh settling in?"

"Oh wonderfully, I believe. She is looking for part-time work while Luca is in school but not having a lot of luck. Do you know of anything?"

I lean my head back against the headboard and groan. Mom's definitely got her matchmaking hat on right now. "We may have something down at the transportation company. Just not sure if she can do it part-time or not."

"If not, we can work something out, maybe I can pick up Luca and keep him after school. She needs to reinvent herself, so to speak."

"What's that supposed to mean, Mom?" I sigh in exasperation. I'm not one hundred percent sure if I want to know what is running through her head at the moment.

"Son, she's lost her husband—one not so good if my understanding is right. She's a single mom, whose whole focus has been on her kid and getting them settled. The only people she's met is us, other than his teachers and the faculty at the school. She needs to interact with people, meet new faces, find her place in her new world. She needs to learn to live again, for herself and not just for that boy of hers."

"Understandable," I tell her, and I do understand where she's coming from. I know what it's like to only live for your kid and not think about yourself. My brothers and mom have been my saving grace throughout the years. "Let's see what we can work out once I get home."

"Thank you, Son, I know you won't regret it."

"I'm sure I won't, Mom, I gotta go, need to get some sleep before I relive this horrible day all over again tomorrow."

"Alright, Son, get some rest, love you."

"Love you too, Mom, give my baby girl a big hug from her daddy."

"Will do," she says as she hangs up the phone. I sit in the bed and think of what we discussed. Caraleigh does need to get out there and meet people, and I know we need an office manager for when the boys and I are away on runs. I worry though, because I really want to pursue something with her, but I have a policy about dating employees. I guess there is an exception to every rule, however, and I'm willing to make one for her so I can see if this is leading where I'm hoping and praying it is.

The next couple of days fly by and it looks like I'll barely make it home in time for the BBQ. From the conversations I've had with my mom, Caraleigh has pitched in with getting things set up. *She'll make a damn good old lady*...I can't help but think to myself. She's a natural and so far everyone that has met her has fallen for her charms. As long as they keep their distance from her their health will stay in good standing. I may not have officially claimed her yet...but she's mine and all those fuckers can stand down. They may not know it yet...but she is officially off the market.

I pull into the yard and see the party is getting started. It's a good feeling to know that while I was away things kept running and there were no major catastrophes I have to put out upon my arrival. My VP—Twisted, keeps things in line, he and his old lady Paisley have been together for years and were both instrumental in getting the Rebel Guardians off the ground and running the way it does now.

"Yo, Axe," I hear called out. Axe is my road name and my brothers are the only ones who use it. I tried to get my mom on board, but even in front of the guys she refuses to use it. She says it isn't the name she gave me and nickname or not, she's using my God-given name. I tried explaining that in the club using my road name is politically correct, but to this day she calls every single one of us by our birth names.

"What's up?" I call out to Hatchet, my enforcer.

"Met Caraleigh and Luca, they're amazing man. That kid is something else, and his momma...wow, what a looker."

"Keep your eyes to yourself, Hatchet, she's not a club slut...she's mine." I know he's goading me, but I can't help respond to his shit.

"You claiming her then?" he asks me with mischief behind his eyes. Hatchet may be one of my closest friends, but he's a shit stirrer at every opportunity.

"Not officially, not yet anyways. Spread the word, she's not up for grabs."

"Uh-huh, you got it, Axe," he says walking away whistling a happy tune, which lets me know he's up to something. I may need to bring my enforcer to his knees in front of the club if he tries something too outlandish.

"Hatchet! Don't start no shit man!" I yell out at his retreating back.

"Wouldn't dream of it, Prez, not one bit." Yet I can still see something behind his eyes which tells me he's lying...*right to my face!*

Looking around I note to myself that her car is not here yet, which means I need to rush through a shower and get the road grime off myself before she arrives and my guys give her shit.

CHAPTER FIVE

Caraleigh

Pulling up to the clubhouse I'm a little nervous. I'm worried about what I'll find, I know that Nan and Braxton say it's a family affair and that they've also invited the employees and their families from the trucking company, but I've read plenty of motorcycle club romance novels, and I know to expect the unexpected. I just don't want my son to be tarnished for the rest of his life at what he may or may not see and witness while we're here. I breathe out a sigh of relief when I notice that women are not scantily dressed. There seems to be no make-out sessions or open displays of sexual encounters, so I get out of the car and go to open the back door to let Luca out.

"Mom, do you see Lily?" he asks me. I look around and don't see her anywhere.

"Not yet, buddy, but she may be inside or out back," I tell him.

He tries to rush out of the car leaving me behind, "Luca! Do not run off young man."

"But Mom..."

"Don't 'but Mom' me mister, we stick together."

"Yes ma'am…" he pouts, not deterring me in the slightest. I don't know all of these people, I've met a couple while helping Nan get ready for this get-together, but that doesn't mean I know them well enough to entrust them with my child's well-being. At least not with him running off on his own, if he were with Braxton or Nan I'd be okay.

I grab his hand and then reach into the car and grab the trays of treats I made to go with today's menu. I love to bake, so I wanted to contribute from myself and Luca. I made iced brownies…without nuts in case someone is allergic… a carrot cake, some no-bake cookies, some lemon bars and peanut butter fudge. I wanted to give everyone a variety to choose from, I'm sure these guys have a sweet tooth…right? Crap, now I'm questioning myself on if I tried too hard.

I hear a booming voice and know immediately it belongs to Braxton, "Hey beautiful, Luca. Come on and follow me around back where everyone is hanging out."

"I have desserts, Braxton, they need to be refrigerated." He whistles loudly causing me to cover my ears and Luca to laugh. I see a guy walking towards us, he has on a vest…sorry, cut as Nan explained to me, he walks closer and I see his name embroidered on the front. It says Chef, I'm guessing this guy likes to cook.

"Yo, Chef, do me a solid and take these trays of dessert to the kitchen and put them in the fridge. I want to take Caraleigh and Luca around back and introduce them to everyone...oh shit, Caraleigh, Luca this is Chef, Chef, my new neighbors and friends Caraleigh, and her son, Luca."

"Nice to meet you ma'am, kiddo. Sure thing, I'll take them and put them away for ya," he says, relieving me of the trays and taking off with no other words said.

"Wow, these guys and their muscles come in handy," I say, joking around.

"Eyes off the muscles, babe, unless it's mine you're admiring," Braxton says to me then adds a wink. I can feel the blush travel from my face down my body, the things he does to me with words and actions alone are terrifying. *If we went any further I wonder what he could do to me.* Jeez, I shouldn't be thinking things like this with my son not even a foot away from me.

"Later, you'll have to tell me what you're thinking about that caused that blush to take hold of your body," Braxton says as he walks away with me and Luca trailing after him. *Yeah, like that's gonna happen, mister!*

"We'll see," I reply. Without warning, I find myself pulled closer to him as he intertwines our fingers together. There's something so...intimate, for lack of a better word...about holding hands. I glance up at him and see him smiling down at me before he gives my hand a squeeze.

"Someday, I'll know all your secrets and you'll know mine," he murmurs. "Now, let me introduce you around."

"I got a chance to meet a lot of them while helping your mom," I say as he walks over to a couple.

"Caraleigh, I'd like to introduce you to my VP, Twisted, and his old lady, Paisley."

"Hey, darlin', how did this brute manage to find someone as beautiful as you to agree to come with him?" Twisted asks, holding out his hand.

"Don't listen to him," the female says as she smacks him on the bicep. "It's a pleasure to meet you, Caraleigh. Is that your little boy?"

"Yes, that's Luca."

"What is he...five, six?" Paisley asks.

"He just turned six."

Paisley turns and lets out an ear-piercing whistle. Within seconds, a little tow-headed boy comes running up saying, "I'm here, Mommy."

"Tig, that little boy over there is Luca. He's the same age as you are so go on now, and introduce yourself, y'hear?" Paisley tells the little boy.

"Another boy? Yippee!" Tig yells, bouncing up and down. "We has too many girls around here today. Sorry, Uncle Axe," he says before rushing off toward Luca.

I'm looking at my son with wide eyes because there seem to be kids everywhere. Mostly girls, but even still, he's got a look on his face that's a cross between excitement and fear. "He'll be fine, sweetheart," Braxton says in my ear. "Nothing will happen to him with all of us watching out."

"Okay, that's good. He's just so shy sometimes," I muse.

"He won't be after today, darlin'," Twisted replies. "You ladies want something to drink?"

"I'm in the mood for a wine cooler, how about you, Cara?" Paisley asks.

"That sounds good."

"You ladies find someplace comfortable and we'll bring them on over."

"C'mon, Cara, let me introduce you to the other women around here," Paisley says, grabbing my arm. It just hit me that's she's calling me Cara...I like it, my own nickname...makes me feel instantly welcome.

As we walk away, I overhear Twisted tell Braxton, "Quiet little thing, isn't she?" I hear the rumble of Braxton's voice, but unfortunately cannot make out his words.

"So, tell me what brings you to our quaint little town," Paisley says once we find a seat in the shade.

"Well, Luca's dad died and I felt it was time for a new beginning," I tell her. "His parents didn't like me and were making my life hell. It was starting to show in Luca's behavior."

"What assholes!" Paisley exclaims. "Oh, thanks, babe," she says as Twisted comes up and hands us each a wine cooler.

"Thank you, Twisted," I tell him, popping the top off and taking a sip. *Twisted*...what an odd and unusual name, I bet there's a story behind that one. As a matter of fact, I notice they all have odd names...note to self, grill Braxton at a later date and time.

"Now, scoot," Paisley says to her old man. "I want to get to know my next best friend."

Her comment makes me laugh and I'm still grinning when I see him lean down and kiss her lovingly before he heads off toward the group of men who are standing around the grills talking.

"How long have you two been together?" I ask, curiosity overriding my normal shyness.

She leans her head back and I can see her thinking before she says, "Holy shit, if you count the fact that he told me in kindergarten he was going to marry me someday, we've been together for twenty-three years now!"

"So did you get hitched on the playground or what?"

Her laughter rings out across the yard before she says, "Oh, you've got a wicked sense of humor. I can see I'll have to be on my toes around you!"

"My mouth tends to get me into trouble," I confess.

"How so?"

"Eh, my in-laws hated that I would speak out, so I stopped doing it. Seems the move has adjusted my thinking."

75

"I hope so. Nan speaks very highly of you," Paisley says.

"She's absolutely wonderful. Luca has started calling her Nan, which is good because my folks live too far away now to see him as often as they used to."

"Do you work?"

I think about her question—I don't *have* to work ever again if I don't want to, but that's not how I was raised. "I did before Luca was born, then became a stay-at-home mom. When Graham got sick, I helped his mother take care of him. Now? Well, honestly, I don't have to work again if I don't want to, but I like the challenge of working, so I'm looking for something, at least part-time."

"You should see if there's anything at the trucking company."

"I can't impose like that," I say, taking another drink from my wine cooler.

"Somehow, I don't think it would be an imposition," she says, looking over my shoulder. Curious, I glance back and catch Braxton watching me. As a blush steals across my face, I turn toward her and shake my head no.

"It's not like that with us, he's my neighbor and our kids are friends."

"Yeah, you keep telling yourself that, Cara," she says causing that damn blush to spread through my body again. Only this time it's accompanied by goose bumps and a shiver that runs down my spine

Braxton

Watching Caraleigh talking and laughing with Paisley has me all tangled up. She's easily the prettiest woman here, and I don't miss the looks all my single brothers have been giving her. In fact, I'm about to make an ass out of myself and beat my chest and claim a woman I haven't so much as kissed...yet, just to keep them from looking her way. Sighing, I turn my attention back to Twisted, who is filling me in on another business we've been looking at buying, only to see his smirk.

"What?" I ask.

"Yeah, just a neighbor, huh?" he retorts. "Thinking you better not take too long to decide what you wanna do with her or one of these other assholes will beat you to the punch."

"Not happening," I growl out. "Hatchet's passing the word. Not ready to claim her yet, but she's not fair game. This lifestyle is new to her, and I want her to adjust and get to know everyone."

"Well, y'know that Paisley will be happy to add to her little girl posse."

"They seem to be getting along rather well," I tell him, reaching down to the cooler and grabbing a fresh beer. "Want one?"

"Yeah, man," he says. Tossing him a cold one, I pop the top and down half of it while surveying the yard. Mom and the other women did a great job setting it all up. Of course, I'm going to have to talk to her about the play area she had built.

"Mom did that, didn't she?" I ask, pointing to the new play area where the kids are running around and screaming.

"Yeah, she said that the kids needed their own space whenever we have barbeques. I happened to agree, so I sent the prospects out to get the stuff and we built it ourselves while you were gone."

"I like it. And the smaller kid-sized picnic tables are perfect as well."

"Hope you keep that mindset when you see what she did inside," Hatchet says, coming up with his own beer.

Shaking my head, I look at my VP and Enforcer and ask, "What did she do inside?"

"Ah, let's show you. I'd rather see your expression," Hatchet says, grinning. "Your woman okay for a few?"

"She's fine, Hatch." Seeing the women have finished their wine coolers, I fish two more out of the cooler and say, "Give me a sec," before walking over to them.

"Having a good time?" I ask her as I hand them both a fresh wine cooler.

"I am, yes, thank you. I love the play area for the kids!" she tells me.

"Seems Mom was busy while I was gone on this latest job," I reply. Paisley starts laughing since she knows how my mom can be when she gets an idea. "Have you seen inside yet?" she asks, still giggling.

"No, headed there now. What time is Donna Jo due?" I ask Caraleigh.

"She should be here any time, but then again, she's horrible with directions so she could also be in Alaska by now. I'll try calling her shortly."

"Okay. Going to see what my mother has been up to inside the clubhouse," I say before dropping a kiss on her head. No, it's not where I want to kiss her but hopefully, it'll keep those fuckers from eyeballing her any more. My intentions have been set in stone where the brothers are concerned.

Caraleigh

He kissed me! Okay, so it wasn't a full-on lips and tongues dueling with me crushed against his body, but still...he kissed me! "You okay, Cara?" Paisley asks.

"What? Oh, yeah, I'm fine, why?"

"You look kind of shell-shocked. I take it that he's not done that before?"

"No! I mean, he's held my hand and all, but he was just walking us home."

"And... he was holding your hand when y'all walked up to us earlier."

"It doesn't mean anything, Paisley. Hell, we haven't even gone out on a date," I say, wishing I could chug the rest of my wine cooler.

"Honey, bikers typically don't date. They see what they want and they go after it," she replies.

"I... see."

"No, you don't but I suspect you will. Just saying, Axe is a helluva good guy. Works hard, loves his daughter and his mom something fierce and is loyal to a fault."

"He seems like a nice guy," I cautiously admit.

"He and Twisted have been best friends forever so I can say with absolute certainty that he is a nice guy. Unless you cross him or hurt someone he cares about and then, all bets are off."

"I'll keep that in mind," I tell her. "Should we be doing anything to help get ready?"

"Now, we've got an hour or so before they fire up the grills and start cooking. All the side dishes are ready. But I want to grab Tig something to drink, you wanna come with me?"

"Sure."

80

Braxton

Walking into the clubhouse, I look at Hatchet and Twisted and say, "Okay, what did Mom do now?"

"Follow me," Twisted says, a grin breaking out across his face. We go through the kitchen and he turns left before we get to the bar.

"All we have are storage rooms down here," I tell them as we start down the hall.

"Not anymore," Hatchet replies, before he bursts into laughter.

Oh for fuck's sake, what did Mom do now? I swear I'm gonna be bald and what hair I have left on my body is going to end up grey! Stopping at the first door on the left, I see a sign on the door where there wasn't one before that says "storage." Raising my eyebrow, I open the door and my jaw drops. When we looked for a clubhouse, we bought an old school and knocked down walls and made it into what we wanted. The kitchen was already an industrial-sized one, but we upgraded the appliances and added a pantry, as well as a walk-in deep freezer. Several of the brothers like to hunt and fish, so we have wild game processed and packaged, in addition to the normal chicken and steak that we all enjoy. But this room here? There are rows of shelves neatly organized with non-perishable items.

81

"What in the hell?" I ask, more to myself than anything.

"Your mom thought it made more sense to be fully stocked for any occasion," Twisted finally says, before bursting into laughter.

"Like what? The zombie apocalypse? Christ on a cracker, that woman is going to make me old before my time," I mutter.

"Christ on a cracker, what are we twelve?" Hatchet cracks up at my verbiage.

"Fuck, don't give me hell," I tell him. "I'm raising a little girl, I can't continuously have the mouth of a sailor...continue," I tell him. When he finally relents from his laughter he does.

"Anyways, there's a method to her madness," Hatch replies. "The grocery store was closing down so she got most of it at a deep discount. Plus, with it being early spring, we'll be cooking out more and shit. It won't go to waste, Axe."

I'm busy counting the cases of paper towels. And toilet paper. We're set if anyone comes down with Montezuma's revenge. Sighing, a grin playing on my lips, I say, "Her heart is in the right place. And, we'll let the prospects keep the inventory up. May as well, right?"

"Oh they're gonna love that," Twisted says. "But wait...there's more," he continues, sounding like one of those game show hosts. I half expect to see a woman in a sparkling gown come forward waving her arms.

We leave the room and he goes to the next door and opens it before standing aside. Taking a deep breath, I walk in and my jaw drops. There are multiple flatscreen televisions with every kind of game system available hooked up on one side of the room, and a long table with laptops on the other wall. "What the hell is this?" I ask.

"She found out that a few of the prospects didn't have their diplomas and said that they had to work toward their GED so they can 'become productive members of society and the club'."

"How is playing video games helping them do that?" I question.

"Oh, they have to earn their playing time. She holds the controllers hostage until they've completed whatever assignment she gives them. Why didn't you mention she used to be a teacher?" Hatch asks.

"Must have slipped my mind," I mutter. "Hell, are the prospects okay with all of this shit?"

"Yeah, actually. Smokey and Bandit have been teaching them computer skills so they don't delete the hard drive, and Law's woman, Ava, has been coming in and helping your mom."

"When does she find time to do this? She watches Lily for me!"

"Oh, she does it while Lily's in school."

"For fuck's sake, I was gone for a *week! Seven-motherfuckin'- days,* how is possible for one person to get all this done in that time frame?" My mother both amazes and shocks me at every turn.

"There's still more, Axe."

"More?" I'm not sure at this point I can handle any more, but I decide to pull up my President boxers and motor on. "Show me."

We head out of the new classroom with me still shaking my head in bewilderment at how my mom managed to accomplish all of this in a mere week. Sneaky woman!

"Okay, you know how we've got a few kids now, right?" Twisted asks.

"Uh, last I saw, we had two. Two children," I reply. "Tig and Lily."

"And... your mom is including Luca in all of this, apparently."

Of course she is, the scheming matchmaker!

"Go on..."

"She decided that the kids needed their own space inside in case we ever have to go on a lockdown."

"A lockdown? What in the everloving hell is she talking about? We've never had to have one. Ever. We're not that kind of club, for fuck's sake." I need a beer. Or ten. Hell, at this rate, I may as well drink a whole case.

"C'mon, Axe, you know we love your mom and if I hadn't agreed, none of this would have happened," Twisted says.

"She must think this club is made of money…" I mutter to myself, causing Hatchet and Twisted to crack up at my supposed joke, which it wasn't by the way. We're doing well financially, but that's just the thing, we are right now, but we need to prepare for a rainy day. I have employees that would like to still be able to feed their families if we ever come into a rough patch.

We go back down the hall and to the other side where she has created two more rooms. The first one is an indoor playroom that is sectioned off to have a small 'house', and then a game area, a craft area, and a video game area. Games and puzzles are neatly stacked on the shelves, along with books. Leave it to Mom to create something like this for the few kids we do have in the MC so far. The second room is a bunk room designed specifically for kids. Along one wall are cribs. *Cribs? Oh for fuck's sake.* "*Why* are there cribs?"

"Wishful thinking on her part? I don't know, man. I mean, right now, I'm the only one with an old lady, and you and I are the only two with kids. Then again, if we have any friendlies visiting, they might have kids, so maybe it's not a bad idea?"

"She also set up a movie room," Hatch blurts out. "But that's for everyone, not just the kids."

"Please tell me she didn't go into our room where we hold church?" I ask. I'm normally a patient man, truly I am, but I think her antics have pushed every last button.

"Nope. But...that's only because Chief stood in front of the door when she tried," Twisted admits.

"That's it, I'm taking her keys away," I mutter, *and her credit cards*, I think to myself. "How in the hell can I command respect when my mother does something like this?"

"Actually, Axe, I approved all of it, and the guys? They're thrilled. They've been around more, hanging out, shooting the shit, that kind of thing. She wanted to start a Sunday movie day, but I told her we had to vote on that," Twisted says.

"Hmm, yeah, like we won't say yes," I reply, looking at all she accomplished. Next thing we'll be having weekly dinners if she keeps this up. In addition to the cribs, she has bunk beds throughout the room, not just the twin-sized ones either. Nope, she has the twin over full-sized bunk beds.

"Tell me we still have our gym?"

"Yep. Although she ordered a hot tub. Said something about it helping our muscles relax once we're done working out."

"I'm taking her credit card away as well."

"Axe, your mom has been more alive this past week than I've seen her in years," Twisted says. He should know. He was there when my dad died and he saw how she grieved. She spent three months making pickles and baking bread. I know when I had her move in with me to help with Lily, she started coming back even more.

"And the guys are all really okay with it?" I ask, running my hands through my hair. Shit, is it falling out? I wonder if Caraleigh likes men who are bald.

"Yeah, man, they really are," Hatch confirms.

"Okay, let me go tell Miss Mischief Maker to slow her roll a little bit. Maybe she can clue me in on what else she envisions for *our* clubhouse so I can bring it to a vote?"

"You can try but she's in her element. Hell, Chef has been singing her praises ever since she put in the garden."

"The...what?"

"Garden. She said fresh veggies and herbs would be good for all of us and you know him, he loves to cook, so he helped her get it planted and everything. Be prepared, man."

"Fuck my life."

Nan

I see Braxton walk out with Twisted and Hatchet and smile. Guess he figured out that I've been a bit busy this past week while he was gone. I just want him and the boys to be comfortable. Maybe if they were, more of them would settle down. Now I need to stay away from him for a little while until he calms down.

87

Walking toward the women, I see Caraleigh and Paisley laughing at something one of the kids is doing and I smile. *She's going to be good for him JB.* I know if anyone knew I still had conversations with my dead husband in my head they'd commit me, but what they don't know won't hurt them, will it? Caraleigh has the sweetest personality, but I know there's a feisty side to her waiting to come out and my son is just the man to make that happen. And that little boy? What a sweetie pie he is! Always looking out for my Lily and so polite. She doesn't know I overheard him talking to Lily one day when he was over playing. If she did, it would break her heart. I know it broke mine. He knew how his father and grandparents treated her and he hated it.

"Lily? Can I tells you something? If I does, can you promises not to tells Nan or your daddy?" he asked.

"I promises," she replied, sticking out her pinky. "Pinky promises, Luca!"

"I misses my daddy because him is in Heaven, but you knows what? Him was mean to my momma all the time. So was my grandparents."

"How was they mean?" Lily asked.

"He would tells her she didn't do things right or that she was fat. Lily, he made her cry!"

"I'se sorry, Luca, that wasn't nice of him even if he was your daddy. Daddies are post to love mommas, right?"

"I thinks so, yes. I don't thinks him loved Momma, though. It's why we moved away, but Momma doesn't know I know."

"How did you find out?"

"I heard my Uncle Chan talking on the phone to my other gramma, the one who loves me. He was really mad when he was telling her what he heard them say to my momma."

"Your momma isn't fat, her is just right! And her is pretty and I likes how she laughs and plays with us."

"I knows! I thinks if my daddy hadn't died, they would have gotten a diborce."

Lily looked at him and he looked back at her before they nodded at each other. "Let's go see if Nan will let us have a smoothie!" Lily said.

I had quickly stepped back and made my way into the kitchen before the kids got in there, and was able to wipe the tears from my face. That poor sweet woman had been degraded by the one person who was supposed to love her unconditionally! Well, if I know anything, and I've lived long enough to learn a thing or two, I can guaran-damn-tee that once my Braxton gets his head out of his ass and makes her his, she'll know what that feels like.

"What has you two laughing over here?" I ask as I sit down with the two younger women.

"Well, Lily was playing by herself since Tig grabbed Luca. When Luca looked over and saw she was by herself, he went over to get her and Tig said something. Luca turned around and told him that it was their job to take care of the girls and Lily was his bestest friend so he was going to play with her too. Tig, instead of getting all huffy? Said okay and the three of them have been playing some crazy game that I think they're making up as they go," Caraleigh said.

"That's sweet of him. You've done a good job, Caraleigh," I tell her. I should know, I raised a good man myself and I see the signs of one in young Luca.

"Thank you. I worry that he doesn't have enough of a male influence though, especially since my brother is so far away now."

"Nonsense, between Braxton and all the boys, he'll get all he needs from them."

"She's right," Paisley said. "These men love kids and of course, now that Tig knows of Luca, I anticipate sleepovers as well."

I'm about to say something when I see Braxton heading in our direction. Time to make my escape. "Gonna run and see if there's anything else to be done before the guys start cooking."

Braxton

I watch my mother scamper off in the opposite direction. She can run but she cannot hide forever. I'm not really upset about what she did. Everything was on my to-do list, I just hadn't gotten to it quite yet.

"We're about to fire up the grills, ladies," I say as I reach Paisley and Caraleigh. She looks so fucking pretty today with her leggings and oversized t-shirt. She looks up at me and smiles. I'm taken back at how her whole face lights up.

"So, did you see what Nan did?" Paisley asks, a grin on her face.

"Yeah and I'm guessing that's why she took off," I reply, before I start chuckling. "Like I won't eventually catch up to her!"

"What did your mom do?" Caraleigh asks.

"She took advantage of the fact I was gone all week and had some things done around the clubhouse that I've been putting off," I tell her. "C'mon, let me show you."

"Okay, I'd like that. I've only really seen the bar and the kitchen."

"You two have fun, I'm gonna keep my eye on the kids," Paisley says as I lead Caraleigh away, my fingers weaving their way between hers.

I don't miss her glance at our hands and I give hers a gentle squeeze. "You okay with this?" I ask, nodding at our hands.

"I... I guess, why?"

"Just curious. I was never much for holding hands but find that I want to hold yours," I admit as I walk us through the back door of the clubhouse.

She starts to giggle when she sees the storage room filled to the brim with non-perishables. The game room has her chuckling. By the time we get to the kids' bunk room, she's laughing so hard she has tears running down her face. "She...she did all this in a *week?*" she stammers out.

"Yep. Give that woman a credit card and keys and she's apparently hell on wheels."

"I'll say. I'm pretty impressed at what she accomplished, to be honest."

"I am too, but I'll deny it if you repeat it," I tell her. "There's one more room, too."

"Another one?"

I nod as I take her into the movie room. "Oh wow, look at this," she says as she walks around the stadium style seats. There are smaller, kid-friendly ones set up in the front with the adult sizes at the back and there are enough that each brother could bring someone. At the back, there's a huge popcorn popper and... wait a minute...oh for the love of all that's holy! A *drink machine?* Caraleigh, seeing the look on my face, starts laughing again and soon, I'm laughing alongside her, with her pressed along my side.

"So fucking pretty," I whisper as I tuck a wayward curl behind her ear and wipe away the tears from her laughter.

She looks down and I use my hand to gently lift her chin so she's looking at me again. "You are, Cara. I'm not the kind of man who blows smoke up anyone's ass, so when I say something, you can believe it's the truth."

"Okay," she quietly says.

Stroking her cheek with my thumb, I lean down until our lips are nearly touching. "Been wanting to do this since the first day I saw you," I murmur before I capture her lips in mine.

Incendiary. The moment our lips touch, I hear her gasp and know that the whoosh I felt go through at our connection was felt by her as well. Her lips are so fucking soft and I find myself pulling her closer so we're touching before I deepen the kiss. "Let me in, sweetheart," I murmur against her lips before I swipe my tongue across her lower lip.

Tentatively, almost as if she's never been kissed before, she opens and I find myself exploring her mouth, tangling with her tongue so intimately that I'm soon groaning low in my throat. This slip of a woman has the power to break me and she doesn't even have a clue. Long delicious minutes are spent learning her, while I fight off the desire to pull her over to one of the recliners and take it further. When I finally need air, I pull back slightly, leaning my forehead against hers as I pepper kisses across her face. "You like that sweetheart?" I rasp out when I feel her shudder against my lips on her neck.

"Mmhmm," she murmurs.

"I did as well," I tell her. Taking her hand I say, "We should probably head back outside. It's about time to fire up the grills."

"Okay," she says, smiling shyly. I love how swollen her lips look and feel like I'm ten feet tall that she's on my arm. She doesn't know it yet, but she's mine.

CHAPTER SIX

Caraleigh

"Mommy!" Luca calls out as we come out the back door. "Where were you?"

"Mr. Braxton was showing me some of the things that Nan did while he was gone last week."

"Did you sees our playground?" he asks.

"Yes I did. Are you having a good time?"

Before he can answer, I hear Donna Jo's voice saying, "I'm supposed to be meeting her here, you big lug!"

Turning, I see that one of the men, I think his name is Boothe, has his arm up to keep Donna Jo from coming any closer. "Braxton? That's Donna Jo and her little girl, Ralynn."

"She's okay to come through, prospect," he calls out. She gives him a dirty look before walking over to me.

"Over-protective much?" she asks Braxton before engulfing me in a hug.

"Sorry about that, but we don't let just anyone on our property," he tells her.

"DJ? This is Braxton Callahan, he's the president of the MC," I tell her.

Her raised eyebrow tells me I've got some explaining to do and I shake my head at her. *Now's not the time.* "Did you have any problems finding it?" I ask.

"Nope. My new GPS system actually gets me from point A to point B," she replies. "It's nice to meet you," she says, turning to Braxton.

"Aunt Cararee?" a little voice says. Looking down, I see Ralynn and I crouch to give her a hug. "Where's Luca?"

"Oh, let me take you over to where he's playing, okay, sweetie?" Taking her hand, I motion with my head for DJ to follow me and walk over to the play area. "Luca? Look who's here!"

"Ralynn!" he screams out, jumping off the swing and running toward us. "You gots to meets my new friends who lives here!" he says, taking her by the hand and running back toward Lily and Tig.

"Paisley? This is my friend, Donna Jo or DJ. DJ? This is Paisley, she's Twisted's old lady and Tig's mom."

"Pleasure to meet you. So Tig is the other little boy running around?" DJ aks.

"He sure is, he and Luca hit it off right away, Luca also has a friend, Lily, who happens to be Braxton's daughter."

"Braxton huh...there's a story I want to hear about," DJ says to me. I know that there will be no sleep until there's a bottle of wine consumed and the complete story of Braxton told. Only problem is,

I don't know exactly what to tell her where it comes to Braxton and myself.

"Later," I tell her and turn to Paisley, only to see a smirk on her face. "What?" I ask her.

"Just curious."

"About?" I put my hands on my hips, taking my mothers pose of, 'don't mess with me' stance.

"Whether or not you're gonna tell the watered-down version you tried spewing to me, or if you'll be real with your girl DJ here."

"Oh, she'll be real with me. She knows better, I will pull it out of her if I have to."

"Wish you two wouldn't talk about me as if I'm not even here. And hey," I pinch DJ's arm, "whose side are you on anyways?"

"Yours, Caraleigh, always yours. But you have to learn to be on your side as well." What in the world does that mean I wonder. "Don't look at me like that," DJ says. "You know what I mean, you always take care of everyone else, would you like me to give examples?"

"No!" I blurt out, like I need all these strangers in my business.

"Oh, I see a girl's night in our future," Paisley blurts out.

"Umm…" I stammer.

"Hell yes!" DJ eagerly agrees. How come I get the feeling I'll be the topic of conversation during this girls night out?

"We should set it up, how long are you in town for, DJ?" They carry on like I'm not even standing here.

"For an undetermined amount of time. I can work from anywhere and Ralynn is homeschooled."

"Give me your number and we can set it up." They exchange numbers and I'm still standing here like a deer caught in the headlights. I look over and see Braxton watching me, he lifts his eyebrows in a silent question wanting to know if I'm okay. I shrug my shoulders and give him a small timid smile, which he returns. Only his smile is bright and does things to me that make my body quiver in anticipation of what's yet to come.

"Earth to Cara," Paisley calls out to me.

"Hmm...what?" I turn my attention back to the girls.

"We were asking what day is good for you so I can set up a sitter for the kids."

"A sitter, why?"

"So we can go out, what happened did your brain fry while looking at Mr. Hottie over there?" DJ, the smartass asks me. I stomp my foot in exasperation, I don't do well with being the center of attention...well, not any more I don't. I used to be the outgoing one, until my deceased husband and his parents got me in their line of fire.

"We're going to have so much fun!" Paisley announces bouncing around on the balls of her feet.

"I don't have many girlfriends, so I'm really looking forward to this."

"Oh joy," I mutter under my breath causing both of them to break out into laughter. I love being the object of attention...not!

"So, girl, tonight I want the whole story of how you met Mr. Hottie pants and explain those smoldering looks he keeps sending your way."

"You're imagining things," I tell her, "you're seeing things where there is nothing to see."

"Whatever you say, Cara," Paisley says, "but I'm not buying that line of bullshit."

"Whatever," I say, because I can't think of anything else to respond to that statement.

"Food's ready," we hear Braxton call out, giving me the perfect out to being the center of attention from my best friend, and her new partner in crime.

"Come on, ladies, let's grab our kids and get their plates made," Paisley says grabbing one of each of our hands and pulling us behind her. "You snooze you lose around here, it's first come first serve, and these guys are animals when it comes to food."

"Hopefully it's not the only time they're animalistic," DJ says winking at me. I notice Hatchet walk up behind DJ, and I know he's fixing to do something to set her ass on fire.

"Not the only time, darlin'," I hear him whisper-shout in her ear, causing her to jump and screech.

Everyone stops what they're doing turning to look and see if there is danger in the area...I'm assuming.

"Asshole!" she screams at Hatchet causing him to laugh.

"Just answering your question, darlin'," he replies with a wink.

"Well, considering I wasn't asking you, maybe you should stay out of other people's conversations and mind your own business!" she huffs out. I can't tell if she's truly upset or not, she has the same look when she's excited as she does when someone's pissed in her cheerios.

"Don't mind Hatchet," Paisley tells DJ. "We don't know what side of the funny farm he was raised on, he always has something smart to say."

"That's because I'm a smartass, darlin'," he replies to Paisley.

"That you are...along with just plain being an asshole."

Hatchet grabs his chest in a dramatic nature, "You wound me, darlin', here I was thinking we were friends."

"Ah," Paisley moves her hand side-to-side, in a sorta gesture.

"Wounded, truly wounded, darlin'," he says as he walks away.

"See, you just have'ta learn how to deal with these guys. You have to think on a five-year-old's level."

"Shouldn't be too hard, since we have kids in that age range," DJ tells her.

"Exactly."

After we get in the long as hell line, get the kids and our plates made and get to the table, I'm utterly exhausted. It's a workout in itself to get the kids wrangled, but when you add grown men who think they're children, it's even more so. I've never met men of this age range that acted more like children than Luca. It's a hard pill to swallow, even for me. The kids are sitting at the kids table and I'm sitting next to Braxton, whose hand has not left my leg since he took the seat to my right. On my left is DJ and next to her is Hatchet. I can hear his attempts at flirting, causing my friend to laugh, which makes me happy. It's been a long time since I've heard her sound so carefree. Across from me are Paisley and Twisted, who has nibbled on her neck and ear as much as he has his food.

I want that someday, I want to experience that kind of deep devotion and love that he shows her...publically! Something I've never felt either. Public displays of affection were a big no-no in my previous marriage. I always felt so isolated and alone, other than Luca, of course. He was my saving grace, my reason to keep living and putting one foot in front of the other, so to speak. *Graham, why couldn't you have ever shown me that I meant something to you?* There was a time that I would've done anything for that man, including losing who I was and who I wanted to be.

"Hey, beautiful, where'd you go to just now in that head of yours?" Busted! Damage control begins in... three...two...one.

"Oh, sorry. I was just thinking of how much I'm enjoying getting to know everyone. I love the vibe of family I'm getting off of everyone here. You guys really are one big happy group. Thank you for letting me, Luca, DJ and Ralynn be a part of this today," I tell him hoping he'll buy that bunch of malarkey I just laid in his lap.

"I'll let you have that play for now," he says as his hand squeezes my thigh. Damn, I thought I'd been pretty convincing personally. I look over to DJ and see she has a look of concern on her face, I must've let my thoughts show pretty drastically for her to be worried. She knows me better than anyone, so she most likely knows where my thoughts were regardless if I tell her the truth or not.

I nod my head at her letting her know I'm good, although it looks like our dreaded conversation tonight will deal with ghosts I'm not in the mood to face. Story of my life, go figure. I wish I could bury the past and keep it there, but the damn thing keeps resurfacing every time I turn around. I mean

Graham is buried, why can't I keep the memories dead with him and move on?

Braxton

I don't like the look on my girl's face, or where her thoughts seem to be taking her. Yes, I said it, my girl, and she is mine. I just have to convince her of that fact and hope she takes it and doesn't try to run from it. Though she won't get far, I won't let her. She was born for me, and I don't let things I want escape my grasp if I have any say in the matter, which in this case I do. I will break down all those walls I see built around her...it's just a matter of time.

As the night progresses, the bonfire is flaming and we have the kids roasting marshmallows. I look over at Caraleigh and her girl posse and see them all laughing being carefree and a sense of calmness and contentment washes through me. This is how it's meant to be...life that is. Not everything is meant to be a struggle. Life is exciting and sometimes downright fucking scary, it's what you make of it that matters most. I plan on making life good for Caraleigh and Luca, they're now mine...my family.

I look around in pride at my brothers, they show me and everyone around them daily what loyalty, drive and commitment mean. They show compassion when it's needed and stand against injustice in the world when required. They may be goofballs, but they're all good men, men I'm proud to have at my back and am honored to stand beside them. When Twisted and I talked about starting an MC, this right here is what I imagined it could be. Family, honorability, faith, loyalty and brotherhood.

We aren't the one-percent club that you typically read and hear about. We don't go out looking for a fight, we don't get into wars over territory. No. Not us. We are about the ride, the wind blowing in your face, the road under your feet and the freedom of the open road. Don't get me wrong, the guys have the capability to get rowdy at times, but every once in awhile, letting off steam is a good thing. I'd rather them have the typical barroom brawl, than be out there being a menace to society. We still fine them if they are out in public and cause problems, we have to in order to keep some semblance of control. But as my mom says...boys will be boys.

I'm sipping on a beer and laughing with my brothers when I feel someone standing behind me. I turn around and see my girl standing there. "What's up, beautiful?" I ask her drawing the attention of everyone around us.

"Hey, it's getting late, I need to get Luca home and in bed. Plus I still have to get DJ and Ralynn settled. The kids are tired and getting cranky. I wanted to come say good-bye and thank you for inviting us, we had a wonderful time." I can't help but smile at the pride I feel of how everyone behaved themselves so she and her friend felt like they are part of the family.

"You're welcome, beautiful, let me walk you and DJ to your cars then if you give me a few minutes to grab Lily I'll follow y'all home."

"That's not necessary, you don't have to leave just because we are."

"I'm not, beautiful, I'm leaving because I'm exhausted and need to get my daughter to bed as well." I look around for my mom and see she's had the same idea and is getting Lily's things gathered up and ready to hit the road.

"Well...alright then," she says and turns quickly away. I watch her ass, mesmerized by the beauty of its plumpness and shape. I bite my tongue to keep myself from moaning out loud. I can't wait to get my hands on it, all of her if I'm being honest. I say goodnight to the brothers I was talking to and make my way to the group the girls are in. I see Twisted has the same idea and is gathering his family up to leave as well. Looks like the evening is winding down and the single men will be the only ones left to bring down the house.

One of my brothers catches my attention and I'm surprised at what I see. Hatchet is standing next to DJ, with a sleeping Ralynn in his arms. Her head is on his shoulder and she looks like she was made to be there...like she's always had a resting place to lay her head. What surprises me the most is how comfortable he looks holding her. DJ has her hand holding his elbow as she waits to be led away. I hope he realizes she isn't a throw away, she's a keeper, someone to be cherished and honored. He isn't known for staying in relationships and I hope this one is different. I don't want any animosity coming between me and my girl. I have a feeling if one of my brothers fucks her girl over, we'll be finished before we even have a chance to begin.

And that is something that is unacceptable. I guess I'll be having a conversation with my brother tomorrow. Hopefully, he's just feeling helpful and it's nothing more than that.

CHAPTER SEVEN

Braxton

The next morning brings me more questions than answers where Hatchet and his feelings are concerned when it comes to DJ. "What do you mean you're confused? You only met her last night, how can you already be unsure?"

"I just don't know, Axe, I mean I'm fighting an extreme attraction to her on every level. Her looks are enough to drop me to my knees, but her sassiness and her personality have me wanting to egg her on one minute and pull her close the next. I desperately want to be buried inside of her. It's unlike anything I've ever experienced before and I don't know what to do with that!"

"So your answer to that is to ask me to send you away on a long-haul run? Since when do you of all people run away from your problems, man? You usually are the first one to stick around and figure things out. I just don't get what leaving will accomplish," I tell him honestly.

"I'm not running away," he growls out at me. "I just need time to sort my head out and figure out what to do next, I've never had this shit happen to me before, give me a break, man."

"I don't know if I'd be doing you any favors by letting you leave. I really think you need to stay here and figure things out, if you don't see her on a daily basis, how will you know what it is you're truly feeling?"

"Fuck!"

"Watch your mouth, young man," Mom says as she enters the kitchen where we've been sitting and talking. "We have a little girl who lives here with ears as big as a wolf and a mouth as big as..."

"Really, Mom, we get it, please don't finish that sentence. I'm enjoying the bubble I live in when it comes to my daughter and the things that are capable of leaving her mouth." I sigh in frustration. She got in trouble at the beginning of the school year for saying 'fuck a duck' when she got an answer wrong to a question her teacher asked her. I got called to her classroom like I'd been the one to say that phrase, one might I mention that she heard from my mother and not from me. It made me feel like I used to when I was young and got called to the principal's office when I'd pull one of my pranks and would get caught. My ass still stings to this day when I think about the ass whoopins I would get from my dad once he'd get off the phone with the school.

I'm brought out of my memories when I hear Hatchet ask me, "What do I do, man?"

"You be a big boy, pull up them britches and face this like a man," comes from Mom.

"Uh, Mom...this is between us, we don't need your matchmaking advice today."

"I beg to differ, Son, I think the two of you need all the help I can give. You're both acting like stubborn fools...do yourselves a favor, march over to that apartment and ask those girls out to dinner. I'll watch the kids...and for goodness sakes, don't say anything stupid and stow the crazy antics, Hatchet. Trust me, no one wants to be on a date with a clown that's escaped the circus," she says as she marches out of the room.

The fuck! Did my mom just demand I go on a double date? This is ludicrous, the nerve of her.

"Dude, Axe-man, did your mom just demand I go on a date with you?"

"Not with me you moron, a double-date with the girls. No wonder she referred to you as the class clown."

"She did not! She referred to me as an escaped clown from the circus."

"Same damn thing, Hatchet."

"So is not!" Is he seriously pouting at me like Lily did when she was two-years old? Something's got to give here.

"Well, I don't know about you, but I'm taking my mom's advice and I'm going over there and asking my girl out on a date."

"Do we date? We're bikers, man, don't we just pound on our chest and demand what's ours?"

"Jesus, Hatchet, you're not Tarzan and DJ is definitely not Jane. Get with the times, dude. This is not a Disney movie special," I say in exasperation as I get up and march to the front door. I turn around to see if he's following me, I smile to myself when I see he is right behind me. He looks like a sullen child that's being led to the library instead of the playground. Little does he know if he plays his cards right it will be the latter for the rest of his life, that is if he can pull his head out of his ass long enough to reap the rewards of what that woman could give him.

Lord only knows I can't wait to reap my own reward. I smile to myself in anticipation, I love to play the game of love and war. Well, more the love part than the war, but I can tell you, the chase is sometimes more rewarding than the actual capture...only I really don't want to chase and play war games with my girl...I'm impatient, and I want her now. I need to make myself so irresistible in her eyes that she doesn't second guess what can be with me. At the same time, I need to be myself so she gets the real me. I'm proud of the man I've grown to become.

As I head over to Caraleigh's, my mind drifts back to last night. *By the time we got back to the complex, all the kids had fallen asleep. Mom had sent me to help Caraleigh with Luca, a task I happily took on. DJ had carried Ralynn into the guest room, telling us good night and leaving me with the woman who was quickly consuming every rational thought in my head. Carrying him upstairs, I followed her into his room and gently laid him down on his bed. She had laughed quietly, saying that once he was asleep, a nuclear blast could go off next to him and he wouldn't flinch. I watched in amazement as she quickly got him undressed and changed into a pair of Paw Patrol pajamas. Then she tucked him in and kissed him, telling him she loved him and would see him in the morning. I wanted that for my little girl—a mom who would tell her those things even if she was sound asleep.*

She had motioned me out of his room and closed his door after turning on a small night light, saying only that since his father had died, he needed one. I had followed her back downstairs and headed to the door when she stopped me.

"Braxton?" she asked.

"Hmm?" I replied, turning toward her. Fucking pretty. So fucking pretty she took my breath away.

"I wanted to say thanks again for today. We had a wonderful time meeting everyone and I know that Luca is thrilled that he met another little boy who lives nearby."

111

I couldn't help myself, I pulled her closer to me until we were chest to chest. "I enjoyed today as well," I murmured. "I know this is fast, Cara, hell it's fast for me too, but there's...something between us and I want to see where it goes."

"I... I don't know what to say, Braxton," she murmured, looking at me with those luscious lips. Lips I was already envisioning around my hardening cock.

"Don't have to say anything, sweetheart," I said, leaning in closer to capture her lips. The earlier kiss had seared her into my memory banks and ruined me for any other woman. She just didn't know it yet.

Deepening the kiss, I let my lips and tongue tell her everything that I couldn't put into words. Her lush, curvy body fit into mine and I wanted to groan at the contact. Her whimpers had me harder than steel and long before I wanted to, I pulled back and kissed her forehead before saying, "I'll call you tomorrow, see what your plans are, okay?"

Breaking myself from my reverie, I realize that we're standing in front of her door. "Well, you gonna knock or what?" Hatchet asks, giving me a knowing look.

"Fucking comedian," I mutter as I reach up and ring the doorbell.

Caraleigh

Sitting in my kitchen being grilled by DJ about Braxton, I'm grateful for the ringing of the doorbell, although I have no clue who could be stopping by. "I'll be right back, hold that thought," I say before getting up and heading to the front door. Looking out the peephole, I'm surprised to see Braxton and Hatchet standing there. *What in the world are they doing here...and together?*

When I open the door, I'm once again struck speechless at the sheer essence of the man standing in front of me. "Hey, Braxton. Hi, Hatchet. What can I do for you guys?" I ask, stepping back to let them both inside.

"Is DJ here?" Hatchet asks.

"She's in the kitchen," I reply, then watch in astonishment as he walks through the living room and back to the kitchen.

"What's going on?" I ask Braxton, who has stepped closer.

"Morning, beautiful," he replies, leaning down and placing a sweet kiss on my lips.

It takes everything in me not to reach up and touch my lips. Or pull his head down, jump into his arms and have my wicked way with him. Right now, it's a toss-up after the kisses I got yesterday. Graham *never* made my body react that way.

113

"Braxton?" I question since he still hasn't answered either of my questions.

"Wanted to see if you ladies would go out with us this evening," he finally says.

"You mean, on a date?" I ask. *Wait, Paisley said bikers didn't date! What the hell is going on?*

"Yeah, on a date," he replies, a grin stealing across his handsome as hell face.

"But what about the kids?"

"Mom said she'd watch Luca and Ralynn."

"Are you sure? I mean, I'd love to go but don't want to put Nan out."

"I'm positive it won't be a problem. Now, was that a yes?" he asks.

"Yes, that was a yes," I tell him, grinning from ear to ear.

"Great, let's go see if your girl is onboard with that as well," he says, grabbing my hand and leading me into the kitchen.

Once we get there I see that Hatchet is sitting next to DJ and she has a smile playing on her lips. "So, are we going out tonight or what?" Hatchet asks, never taking his eyes off my best friend.

"We are, yes," I reply. "Would either of you like some coffee?" I've got to keep my hands busy or else I'll just grab onto the handsome hunk standing next to me. Focus Caraleigh, focus!

"We've got time before we have to head down to the trucking company," Braxton says, going over to my coffee pot and grabbing two mugs from the cupboard above it. I see DJ's eyebrows raise and shake my head no. Going to the fridge, I pull out creamer and set it on the table. I'm not one for coffee—give me a diet soda or a Dr. Pepper and I'm raring to go, but my girl loves her coffee so I've always had a coffee pot.

"Where are we going?" DJ asks as she sips her coffee.

Braxton brings over the two cups, placing one in front of Hatchet, before sliding into the chair next to me after he moved it closer, that is. "I was thinking about the Barnhouse in the next town over, it has dancing, and the best steak you could sink your teeth into, if that's good with you two?" he asks, stirring in some creamer.

"But it's a school night," I say.

"No, it's a school holiday tomorrow," he replies.

"Already?"

"Yeah, Labor Day," he says.

"Well hell, I guess moving and getting settled got me all turned around. And you're sure Nan doesn't mind?"

"Nope, in fact, she's going to bring Lily over here so if the kids get tired, they can all go to sleep and be comfortable."

"What time do you want to go?"

"We'll come get you around six if that's okay?"

"That'll give us enough time to feed the kids," I muse.

"Don't bother. Mom is planning to make them homemade pizza," Braxton says. "She also informed me that you're looking for a job?"

"Yeah, I am hoping for something part-time but the only thing out there is at the convenience store."

His look stops me and I immediately realize that there's no way in hell I'll be working at a convenience store. "We need help down at the trucking company," he blurts out.

"What kind of help?"

"Someone who can do the books, schedule the runs, make sure the shit is straight for the accountant, that kind of thing."

"I know how to do those things."

"Great, come in Tuesday and we'll get your paperwork sorted."

"Are you serious?" I ask. "I mean, I haven't worked in years, Braxton." I knew he was a jump into it kind of guy, but seriously a job? Without even checking past employers, or checking on what I majored in at school? Usually a potential employer likes to do reference checks...don't they?

"Positive. It won't take you long to get up to speed."

"So, you got any other jobs available?" DJ asks.

"What?" I question, looking at her. She had mentioned moving closer to me but right now, I'm a bit slow so her asking that has me looking at her all crazy-like.

"You know I wanted to move closer, just need to find something and a place to live."

"As a matter of fact, we need someone to oversee the complex here," he tells her. "And one of the perks is a place to live. But I thought Cara said you homeschooled Ralynn, and that you wrote books?"

"Well, I homeschool her because of the area I currently live in, and I can write anywhere and any time."

"You want to see the place?" he asks her.

"Now?"

"No time like the present," he replies.

"Sure, why not?" she tells him, standing up. "I'll go slip on some shoes."

I'm sitting at my kitchen table looking at the three of them as if they've popped out of an episode of the Twilight Zone. How did I go from yakking with her about Braxton and how we were doing with the new move to having a job and her relocating? "You okay, sweetheart?" he asks.

"Hmm? Yeah, I'm good. Gonna go get my shoes on, be right back."

Braxton

117

While we wait for the two women to return, I look at Hatchet and see a goofy grin on his face. "What's the look for, man?" I ask him. He contributed nothing to the conversation yet is acting like the cat who caught the proverbial canary.

"Ah, just thinking that life is looking pretty good right about now," he replies. "You done with that?" he asks, motioning to my coffee cup.

Now I'm feeling as if I've dropped into a parallel universe. Hatchet is a lot of things but domestic? Not in this lifetime, despite Mom's constant 'badgering' at the clubhouse. "Yeah, man, thanks."

"No, thank you. You managed to move that delectable DJ a helluva lot closer so I can see where it'll go."

"Does this mean you no longer want a long-haul run?"

"Nope, don't want it...not even close."

"Don't fuck that up, man. She's not your usual bang and go and if you mess that up, you might screw things up between me and Cara," I warn him.

In the middle of rinsing out the cups and putting them in the dishwasher, he throws back his head and laughs, making me want to throat punch him. Only, should I do that to someone who is one of my best friends? Something to think about I suppose.

The girls enter the room with the kids following in their wake. "Morning, buddy," I say to Luca.

118

"Mornin', Mr. Braxton, Momma says Ralynn and I has to get our shoes on because you're taking us to looks at anothers apartsment."

"Sure am, buddy, seems DJ and Ralynn will be moving into an apartment of their own."

"Possibly!" DJ shouts out. "Let's not get their hopes up in case it doesn't work out," she says to me sternly. Yeah right, as if I'm not going to do everything in my power to make sure she stays here...not just for Cara, but for Hatchet as well.

"It will work out, trust me," I tell her.

"Yesss!" Luca screams out, punching his fist in the air. Seems I've made someone else's day as well. Looks like he'll have two little girls to watch out for instead of just my girl.

We head to my apartment so I can get the master key I have to the unit I have in mind for DJ. She will be close to me and Cara instead of on the other side of the lot. It's the only one I have left that's close by. It's a three bedroom, but I think it will work out well for her. I'm envisioning her using the spare bedroom for an office. Every writer needs their own space to create their masterpieces. *Man, it must be hard to put yourself out there like that.* I don't think I'd personally be brave enough to do it myself. The criticism alone would be enough for me to hunt down the asshole and pummel their face until they retracted any hurtful words. Yeah—nope, I couldn't do it...no way, no how.

As I open my front door I'm met with a bundle of energy—my daughter. "Hey, baby girl," I say as I pick her up and give her a kiss to the top of her head and snuggle her to me for a hug.

"Hi Daddy, I misseded you."

"You did huh, I wasn't gone long."

"Longs enough," she huffs out at me causing me to laugh at her statement. My little girl is having some separation anxiety from me being on the road for so long. I hold her closer, not looking forward to the day I won't be able to do this anymore and she will care less how long I'm gone for. It breaks my heart to even think about that day.

"I got an idea," I tell her. "I'm taking DJ and Ralynn to look at an apartment, you wanna come with us?"

"You betcha," she says wiggling to be let down.

"Hurry up, everyone is waiting out in the hallway on us," I shout at her retreating back.

"Two shakes," she yells back. Where she comes up with the stuff that leaves her mouth sometimes stuns me to the point of silence. I mean, what is there to say to that? Not even two minutes later she's running down the hall in mismatched clothes with flip-flops in her hands.

"Did you even brush your hair?"

"No times. Let's go, Daddy." No time? I would've made time for it. Before I can say anything she's ripping open the front door and making her way to where Luca and Ralynn are standing next to Hatchet. "Uncles Hatch!" she screams out and launches herself in the air into his open arms. She takes a few years off my life every time she does this with one of the brothers. She just expects them to catch her, never checking first to see if their hands are otherwise occupied. One day one of them won't catch her and my fear is that she will be physically hurt.

"Always check before you jump up expecting someone to magically catch you Lily! You just scared ten-years of your dad's life little girl."

"Sorries, Daddy," she says hanging her head down.

"You're not in trouble, you just scared me baby girl." She reluctantly climbs down Hatchet's body and goes over to her friends. Her dejected look is making me feel like a real jackass, but I have to make sure she thinks about her safety first—always. Anything happens to that little girl and my world would be shattered beyond repair. As my heartbeat slows back to an acceptable rate, I start walking towards the unit. I can hear the kids chatting away behind me when a hand grabs mine and fingers intertwine with mine, and I instantly calm. She does that for me, centers me and makes me feel ready to take on the world.

"You did the right thing you know? If we don't call them out on their actions nobody else will, it's our job as parents to sometimes be the bad guy, even if it isn't our intention to do so. No one will ever love or look out for our kids like we will. Don't be so hard on yourself, Braxton, in five minutes or so she'll forget that the incident even took place. Kids are resilient you know?"

"I know, it still breaks my heart to know I'm the one that put that look on her face though."

"Trust me, if anyone understands that feeling well it's me. Ever since Luca's dad died, I've had a hard time with the discipline. I feel like I somehow owe him to be easier on him. In my head and heart though, I know if I do that he won't ever learn. We have to stand firm with our kids and show them the errors of their ways. It's how they grow and learn."

"You're right, logically I know that here," I say pointing to my head. "But in here," I point to my chest, "I feel like I owe her something more, with her not having a mother and all." I stop talking as we step in front of the door, using my key I open it up and step back allowing everyone to enter before I do. This particular unit had been planned for my family, only when we needed to move in it wasn't ready so I moved into one that was as close to a floor-plan as the one I designed for us. When you walk in, this one is more of an opened up apartment. You walk straight into the living room, the kitchen is to the left, and the first bedroom is directly to the right. You walk down the hallway and there is another door, it connects to a bathroom which is in Jack and Jill style connecting the two bedrooms. Next door on the right is the second bedroom, further down directly at the end of the walkway is the master bedroom. It's huge and has a walk in bathroom that contains a spa tub, along with a stand-up shower with a bench. I had designed it big enough for my large frame to fit in.

After everyone does a walk through I ask, "Well, what do you think? Will this work for you and Ralynn?" I'm hoping that DJ has fallen in love with it.

"Braxton, this place is breathtaking, are you sure I shouldn't be paying for such luxurious accommodations?"

"No, it's a perk of your job, you won't get paid as much as you would at another management position because your rent and utilities are included with the job title you will be carrying."

"Wow, this is the best job perk anyone could receive, I am still feeling guilty about how excited I am. I accept your job offer and the apartment if you're completely sure."

"I'm positive, I need people behind me that I trust."

"But I don't understand, you don't know me, how is it you're willing to trust me so easily?"

"Call it a gut instinct. I know it's Sunday and all, but Hatchet and I really need to get to the shop. We're behind in orders and paperwork. If you are ready, I will get keys to you and you can fill out the necessary paperwork in the morning."

"Is this really happening?" she asks out loud.

"Sure is, darlin'," Hatchet tells her. "Congratulations, we'll talk about getting your belongings moved down here and getting you set up." As he wraps that up we each grab a kid and head out the door.

CHAPTER EIGHT

Caraleigh

Later that evening finds me and DJ in my room getting ready for our double date. We've already picked out our outfits for the night. I chose a flowy skirt with a large printed flower pattern. I'm pairing it with a cream colored, button down blouse and my cowboy boots will add to the outfit. Make it more country like, the outfit makes me feel beautiful and ready to take on the night. DJ is wearing a pair of skinny blue jeans that look like they've been painted onto her skin. She's pairing it with an off the shoulder rose-colored sequined blouse. She looks stunning in this outfit, and to be honest I'm a little envious of the way she looks. My girl is naturally beautiful and takes pride in herself. Not that I don't, I just naturally have more curves that never go away no matter how hard I've tried.

We have our make-up done to perfection, we both have chosen to wear our hair down, DJ is wearing hers straight, but I've added large curls to mine to add body. It's in beautiful ringlets that fall over my shoulders and down my back, just over my shoulder blades. The kids are dressed in their pj's for a night with Nan and Lily. We loaded a backpack down with kid movies, microwave popcorn and a few extra little treats. Nothing that will overly sugar them up, but enough to keep them out of Nan's hair for a small amount of time.

DJ has one of her paperbacks that she has packed, although that's a special treat for Nan and shouldn't be read by anyone under the age of eighteen, it's full of sexy goodness. She's been talking about getting one of her books on her e-reader. DJ wanted to do something special for her though since she's going to be watching our kids for us tonight as a favor, that benefits us a lot more than it does her. I hear a knock on the door and go to the living room to open it. Luca and Ralynn are standing next to the door, and Luca is already wearing the backpack. I'm guessing they're excited about their sleepover with Lily tonight. Sometime throughout the day, this turned from Nan watching the kids while we went to dinner over here, to the kids staying the night at their house.

Who am I to argue, I trust Nan and Braxton, so it was easy for me to agree when she sent me a message earlier asking if it'd be alright. Why she'd want all those kids for that long... willingly, is beyond me. The three of them are already a bundle of energy...add the three of them together and it's like a nuclear explosion waiting to happen. She's a braver woman than I am, that's for sure. Although if I'm being honest with myself, I see sleepovers here at some point in time. Something that I'll make sure

I have an unopened bottle of wine handy for such a time.

"You two excited to sleep over at Lily's tonight?" I ask them, even though I can already see the answer to my question. I hear the knock at the door again...shit, I can't believe I forget they were at the door. The kids just look so cute I couldn't help but stop and interact with them. What can I say, their eagerness is catching.

"Coming," I call out so they know I heard them. I look out the peephole just to verify that it's who I think it is and my breath catches. Damn, Braxton is so stunning that I can't catch my breath, nor figure out what to say. "Damn girl, get your shit together!"

I stand straight, wipe my hands down my skirt and take a deep, much-needed breath and open the door. I place a smile on my face. "Hi, guys, wow— don't you both look handsome," I say to them, meaning every word.

Braxton moves closer and leans down, kissing my cheek as he whispers, "You're gorgeous," causing a blush to creep over my face. Looking down at Luca and Ralynn, who are practically bouncing up and down, he says, "You two ready?"

"Yess!" they both scream, making me laugh. I've always thought each age Luca was at was the perfect one, but right here and now? It's the perfect age.

"We gots snacks and everything and I already told Momma and Aunt DJ that I would protects

Ralynn and Lily while you was gone," Luca says. Braxton musses his hair and grins at his words. "Wouldn't expect anything less, little man," he tells him. "You ladies ready to go?"

"Yes, let me grab my purse and call DJ down," I say, walking toward the stairs. "DJ? The guys are here so get a move on!"

"Hold your horses!" is yelled down the stairs, making me shake my head as I grab my purse off the side table.

Minutes later, DJ appears from upstairs, earning a low whistle from Hatchet. Looks like I need to keep an eye on things and maybe grill her for a change!

We walk over to Braxton's house, and the kids are holding hands again. I notice once again that Luca has himself on the outside near the parking lot. He's always been protective of her and I'm glad to see that he's the same way when he's with Lily. *He's going to be an awesome man when he grows up.*

Once we have the kids dropped off, Braxton leads us to his huge-ass truck and I start laughing. "How in the hell am I supposed to get up in there?" I ask between my giggles.

"Just watch," he tells me, a grin playing across his face. He unlocks the door and hits a button and a set of stairs come down so I don't have to take a running jump and pray I make it. As I'm stepping up, I feel his hands at my waist and warmth

128

instantly suffuses my body. "Let me help," he murmurs as he gets me settled in the front passenger seat before he pulls the seatbelt out and stretches it across my chest until it clicks. Everywhere his hand has touched, even the glancing ones, feels like tiny sparks of electricity and I have to close my eyes and take a deep breath to calm my raging hormones. It's obviously been too long if just a mere touch has me lighting up, but then again, I'm beginning to suspect it's the man, not the length of my dry spell, that has me reacting this way.

"Y'all in?" he asks once he's in the driver's seat.

"We're good," Hatch replies.

Braxton

She looks stunning and whatever perfume it is that she's wearing is subtle yet intoxicating. Grateful that it's somewhat dark in the cab of my truck, I discreetly adjust myself, a condition I'm becoming all-too familiar with where she's concerned. I suspect whether I have her once or a million times, my reaction will always be the same. Tonight, she has her hair in fat curls that go down her back and I just want to see them splayed out over my chest as she rides me. *Down, boy!*

"So the food there is pretty much what you'd expect at a steakhouse. Chicken, several different fish, and of course, steak. The fish is seasonal if memory serves, isn't it, Hatch?" I ask.

"Yeah, they usually have salmon and tilapia, but depending on the time of year, they'll have rainbow trout and even lobster."

"Really?" she asks. Unable to help myself, I reach over the console and snag her hand.

"Yep," Hatch replies, "and they usually have a live band on the weekends. They play country covers and sometimes, older pop ballads. It's anybody's guess, actually. Nice place, though."

He goes back to talking to DJ, leaving me to my date in the front seat. I mentally snort at that thought. The last time I dated was in high school. No time for it when I was in the military and when Twisted and I decided to start up the MC, women were falling over themselves to be with a biker. A little bit of guilt tickles my subconscious. I wasn't exactly a manwhore before Daria or even after she left, but I've definitely had more than my fair share of women. I hope that's not a problem for my woman. I know from what she's shared and how she reacts that Graham was likely her one and only, and I'm sure that has a lot to do with her lack of self-confidence where we're concerned. Gonna break her of that habit.

"What's the dress code at the trucking company?" she asks, interrupting my reverie.

"Honestly? Pretty much anything goes as long as the important parts are covered. Jeans, leggings, dresses, skirts—doesn't matter to me at all," I tell her.

"You may have to change that once you get bigger," she says.

"What do you mean?"

"Well, keep in mind I've not seen anyone who works there except for you, of course, but everywhere I've ever worked has always had a dress code of sorts to prevent anyone from wearing booty shorts to work."

Hatch interrupts, saying, "What's wrong with booty shorts?"

She turns to look at him and replies, "Nothing, but there's a time and a place for them and an office environment isn't either one. But, you're the boss, so whatever you say is fine. Just wanted to make sure I didn't need to go shopping tomorrow."

"Tell you what, you see what you think and if you feel we need to create a dress code, I'll take it under advisement," I tell her, giving her hand a squeeze. The smile she gives me lights up the cold dark places in my heart. I want to own all of her smiles.

As our drive continues, I point out various points of interest to her, making mental notes of where I plan to take her on our next outing. Yeah, I may be moving fast, but life is too short to stay stagnant. Now to get her onboard with my plans.

Pulling into the parking lot, I hear her gasp of surprise and grin. The Barnhouse is one of the biggest steakhouses around, with a two-story barn that features the bar and dance floor downstairs, and the restaurant upstairs. I stop at the front of the building and put the truck in park, hopping out to let the women and Hatch out before I park. There's no way I want her walking too far. "I'll be right back, Cara," I murmur.

"Okay, Braxton. We'll wait for you," she says, a smile lighting her face once again.

DJ

I watch my best friend's face light up when he says he'll be right back and internally grin. She has no idea I know just how bad it got for her, but I read between the lines. She's never had anyone like him in her life and I know, even having just met him, that he would move the sun in the sky if she asked him. Looking up at my date, I smile and say, "So, handsome, what do you do for the MC?"

"I'm one of the drivers at the trucking company."

"So you go out of town too?"

"I mostly handle the short runs, but yeah, I occasionally have a longer haul. Don't you worry

132

your pretty little head, though, I'll get you moved. How soon you want to do it?"

My mind is still reeling over the fact that I have a job and a new place to live. These men move fast. "I'm living in a family-owned rental, so as soon as I get packed, I can move."

"Would two weeks be enough time? I'm sure Cara can help do any of the office stuff for the complex until you get here."

"Yeah, I can help if Braxton shows me what needs to be done," she says, looking at me with wide eyes.

I don't want to appear too eager, but I've missed Cara and I know Ralynn and Luca have missed one another as well. The fact that we'll be in the same complex is great and even if whatever this is with Hatchet doesn't work, it won't impact our friendship. We've been through hell and high water together. "I'll double-check my calendar and make sure I'm not coming up on any deadlines. You know how I get when those are looming."

Cara bursts into laughter. She's been around for every one of my books, offering her opinion, proofreading and at times, editing, although she claims she isn't good. "Yeah, Hatch, are you sure you want this sleep and shower-deprived female moving here? When she's on a deadline, it's a miracle that Ralynn eats!"

"Hey now, it's not that bad!" I exclaim as Braxton walks up to us having finally parked.

"What's not that bad?" he asks, taking Cara's hand to lead us inside.

"How DJ gets when she's close to one of her deadlines," Cara tells him.

"What?" I ask. "I mean, doesn't everyone survive on caffeine and nicotine and Ramen noodles when their back's against the wall?"

"Uh, no," Cara says, smirking.

I'm about to reply when we reach the hostess station where the little snip of a girl is eye-fucking both men. Good thing for her that they seem to be oblivious, I'd hate to chip my polish scratching her eyes out.

Braxton

"Did you have a reservation?" the teenaged girl asks.

"Yes, under Callahan," I reply, pulling Cara closer. I can't believe the nerve of this chick and feel like I need to take a shower after she finishes running her eyes up and down my body.

Before I can say anything, Cara leans in and says, "You might want to watch your eyes, honey. Some women might take offense to you eye-fucking their men in front of them."

Holy fucking shit! My girl's got some sass! And... the hard-on that I had willed away thinking about polar bears and glaciers? It's back. Fuck my life.

"I'm sorry?" the hostess questions. As if she didn't know exactly what Cara was talking about!

"She's a lot more polite than me, sunshine. So I'll be a little clearer, okay? Their eyes are not below their belts," DJ says. And... not that I'll look, but I'm sure Hatch is in the same predicament I am right about now.

"Is there a problem, Braxton?"

"Hey, Gino, yeah, we've got an issue. Or rather, our women have one."

"What seems to be the problem, ladies?"

"Your hostess was rudely eye-fucking our dates," DJ replies. "Totally inappropriate and I would apologize for the language, but there's no other word for what she was doing. It's not only unprofessional behavior, but it's rude."

"Alicia, we've discussed your unbecoming behavior before. Clock out. You're done here," Gino tells the teenager. "My apologies, ladies, will you follow me?"

I'm blown away. I met Gino when we first came to Corinth to check into things and he was instrumental in the MC finding the schoolhouse that we converted to our clubhouse. He loves to ride but declined the invitation to join the MC, saying he was too old. But, we get him out for the runs we do

135

and he has a good time which is all that matters. "Gino, is that necessary?" I quietly ask him. "She's just a kid, likely working to earn mall money and shit."

"Unfortunately, your women are not the first to complain about her behavior towards their dates. That is not the kind of atmosphere we wish to convey here at The Barnhouse. She was warned that the next complaint would result in her termination."

"I'm sorry," Cara softly says. "I hate that she was fired because of us."

"She was fired because of her behavior," Gino replies. "Now, please, enjoy your evening here, I would like your honest input."

Cara smiles at him as he pulls the chair out for her, saying, "Thank you, Gino."

"You're most welcome, pretty lady," he replies before pulling out DJ's chair for her.

While we wait for the server to bring us menus and take our drink orders, I lean in close and whisper, "You have no idea how your sassy mouth turns me on." The blush that covers her face has me grinning before I tuck one of her wayward curls behind her ear and drop a kiss on her temple. I am going to wear her down one way or another, that's for sure.

"Braxton?" a male voice asks.

I look up and see Gino's son, Stephan. "Hey, Stephan, your dad has you working, huh?"

"Yes, sir. What can I get for you to drink?"

"Ladies, they've got a black raspberry frozen margarita that is really good," I say.

"I'd like to try one," Cara replies. "Can I also have an ice water?"

"Make that two, please," DJ interjects.

"What about you two gentlemen? And do you want me to tell you the specials for the evening or just order off the menu?" Stephan asks.

Because I'm driving, I won't drink, so I say, "Sweet tea, Stephan."

"I'll take whatever you have on tap," Hatch adds.

"Can we hear the specials?" Cara asks. I listen to his spiel already knowing I want the surf and turf. Maybe if she gets something different, we can share?

"It all sounds so good," she says, looking at me. "What are you getting, Braxton?"

"I usually get the surf and turf, sweetheart. If you have a taste for something else, we can always share."

"The parmesan-crusted chicken looks good and so does the grilled shrimp."

"Well, if you're game, I'll get what I generally do, you get that and we'll share between us," I tell her. "Fair warning, though, I don't share my asparagus."

She starts laughing and says, "It's all yours, handsome. I don't care for asparagus that much. They've got grilled green beans so I'll go with those and yes, I'm okay with sharing since I like steak and lobster as well."

Once DJ and Hatch order, we sit back and wait for our drinks to arrive. I'm enjoying being out with my woman. Thinking back to Daria, I realize that I was never in love with her, more in love with the idea of having something that was just mine. She wasn't happy when she got pregnant and until she left then finally divorced me, I remained faithful. Hell, she terminated her parental rights to Lily, something that still blows my fucking mind. At least, if this goes where I'm hoping, Cara can adopt Lily so we all have the same last name. I made up for that four years of celibacy as soon as I got the final documents, going through women so fast that even my mom was appalled. But no one, until Caraleigh, had captivated me to the point I was making long-term plans, at least in my head. I could picture her lush curvy body beneath me, flushed with desire and passion. Swollen belly holding a child we had lovingly created. Teaching my daughter and her son and any children we had everything they needed to know to become fine, upstanding citizens.

I'm brought out of my thoughts when Stephan returns with our drinks. I'm anxious to see what Cara thinks of the drink. I know it's one of Mom's favorites which is why I recommended it to her and DJ. Seeing she has taken a sip, I ask, "What do you think?"

A beaming smile turns my way and she replies, "It's delicious! I usually like strawberry margaritas, but this is a great addition to the adult beverages I am willing to drink."

"Glad you like it, Cara," I tell her as I drink some sweet tea.

A different server brings out our salads and we start eating. I'm watching her, paying attention to every little thing she likes and when they bring out the warm honey wheat bread, I take the cutting board and slice it before asking, "Which part of the loaf do you prefer?"

"Don't laugh but I like the 'bread butts' on loaves like this, even though I throw them away on regular loaves of bread!"

I can't help it—I start laughing. She's so damn serious and the earnest look on her face has me enraptured. "I told you not to laugh," she says, lightly touching my arm.

"Honey, that's kind of funny if you think about it."

"How so? On this kind of bread, you put on butter and it melts in and gets all gooey and yummy. Regular bread does not do that at all."

As our dinner progresses, the conversation flows and I find out more about the woman I have my eyes set on. Once we receive our entrees, I take the extra plate and cut half the steak for her, then break the lobster tail and scoop out half the meat. "Braxton, that's too much!" she exclaims, even

139

though she's done the same with her chicken and shrimp for me.

"Whatever you don't finish, we'll take home." No big deal. If she wanted both meals, I'd let her have them.

"Okay, if you're sure," she replies, handing me my plate.

Once dinner is done, I'm eager to head downstairs to dance, wanting to feel her close to me. Seeing Stephan approach, I motion for the check and he crouches down next to me. "Dad said that tonight is on the house for the earlier problem you had."

"Can't do that, Stephan. We've got drinks on the bill as well."

"You can take that up with him, I'm just the messenger. He wanted me to ask if you wanted dessert served up here or down on the dance floor? He has a booth set aside for y'all."

Fuck me. How did I get so lucky? "Yeah, we'll do that, can we order it down there or what?"

"Either one, he's told the waitress at that section that the drinks are on the house as well, so whatever you decide, just let me know."

Hatch, catching onto what Stephan is saying, pulls out his wallet and pulls several twenties out and hands them to Stephan. "What's this for?" he asks.

"Just because your dad is comping everything tonight doesn't mean we don't take care of the

140

waitstaff," Hatch tells him. I give him a chin lift because he's correct. We aren't stiffing our waiter or the waitress downstairs just because everything is on the house tonight.

Caraleigh

When we get downstairs, Gino leads us to the booth he's had reserved for us. With a nod to the waitress, he leaves us to settle in. "I can't believe he did that for us," I say to the table.

"He didn't have to, but it's much appreciated," Braxton says. "You want another of those drinks?"

"You mean heaven in a glass frosted with sugar? Yes please," I reply. They're so yummy but I need to be careful. I've never been much of a drinker and I don't want it to go to my head. Hopefully, a full tummy will help. Plus, he did mention dancing. Another good thing to add to this scenario is that I don't have to wake up to a rambunctious little boy in the morning, who knows, maybe I will let my hair down a little tonight and have some much needed adult fun.

As our waitress sets our drinks down at the table she compliments my skirt and tells me how much she loves my boots. DJ and I talk fashion with her for a few minutes before she's pulled away by

141

another customer calling out for her. She seems like such a lovely woman, someone DJ and I could definitely become friends with if given the time. She was so down to earth and funny, she told us funny stories about patrons and some of the things she's witnessed. As she walks away, Braxton grabs my hand to get my attention, "I've been dying to get you on the dance floor, Cara. I want to hold you in my arms as we sway to the music...what do you say, care for a dance, sweetheart?"

"I would love to," I tell him. I hope my excitement is showing with my smile. I want him to know how he makes me feel with my actions instead of words. Because words are just that words...they can be used for lies and manipulation and I would rather show him with my actions what he's become to mean to me. When we get out on the dance floor, there is a slow song playing. Braxton pulls me in his arms, places one hand on my hip and the other around my shoulders. We lazily sway at first, then he pulls moves that I wasn't expecting. Next thing I know he's waltzing me around the floor to a country and western song. One I haven't heard before, but it's a beautiful ballad.

The next song is a faster pace, I'm surprised at how well my man can dance...wait a minute, backup there a second, Cara...your man, since when? I get swung out and pulled back in which immediately gets me out of my head. The next thing I know we're dancing, laughing and all my troubles

142

disappear. DJ and Hatchet are dancing next to us and we're all having so much fun that I already regret when the night will come to an end. If I could stay in this moment for eternity, it would be the most rewarding time spent here on earth. I could die a happy lady and look back with no regrets. Holy shit! What has me thinking these crazy ass thoughts? This is not me, I'm down to earth Cara, I don't daydream, I don't think outside of the box. I'm always the level headed one, the one that keeps everyone else around me grounded and on track. I need to get my head out of the clouds and enjoy my time with Braxton, but at the same time keep reality from becoming fantasy.

"You ready to sit down and get some refreshments, beautiful?" he asks and I nod my head in agreement. I've worked up quite the thirst twirling around the dance floor, not to mention I think I feel sweat dripping where it's not meant to be.

"Yes please, but first I need to visit the ladies room."

"I'll come with you," DJ calls out to me. "All that maneuvering on the dance floor has jiggled the bladder and it's begging for a release," she says to me as we make our way. She always says the craziest things that make me laugh. I haven't had so much fun in years! We each take care of business and meet at the sink. As we wash our hands we look up at the mirror at the same time and burst out laughing...not sure what's funny but I'm willing to go with it.

"Are you having fun tonight, DJ?"

"I am having an amazing time. Hatchet is a trip and he makes me laugh and smile," she says with a huge grin covering her face. "What about you, Braxton doing it for you still?" she asks, teasing me, she knows he is she's just being a nosey bitch.

"I don't think I've ever had this much fun on a date before." That's kind of sad if you think about it. I was a married woman and Braxton makes me feel more alive than Graham ever did.

"If anyone deserves it, you do," she tells me as she applies more lipstick. I've never been one to wear it, preferring a flavored lip gloss instead, which I quickly reapply.

"I really like him, DJ. But don't you think it's all moving a bit too fast?" I ask her.

"I don't think so at all and anyway, isn't that for you and him to worry about?" she fires back.

"I guess so. I'm just worried because it's not just us, we've both got kids to think about."

"Well, from where I'm sitting, that man's on a mission and you're going to find yourself wedded and bedded or vice versa before you know it!" she says before closing up her purse. "You ready?"

I'm still processing her last words. *Wedded and bedded?* A man like him that could have anyone isn't going to want to saddle himself to a woman like me who has the sagging boobs and stretch marks from a child. I refuse to get my hopes up. Putting a smile on my face, I say, "After you!"

Braxton

While we wait for the women to return, I look at Hatch and say, "Need to send a text out so we can have church on Monday. Get the runs set up for the next week, figure out how we can stop Mom from doing any more at the clubhouse, and I'm going to call for a vote about making Cara my old lady."

His eyebrows raise as he sips his beer. "Kinda fast, ain't it?" he asks.

"Nope. I can feel it down to my bones that she's the one. But, need to make sure that the brothers are okay with it before I ask her if she'll be my old lady, y'know?"

"She'd make a good one from what I can see," he muses. When he stands up, I turn my head and see the women coming back. Standing up, I let Caraleigh get into the booth before I sit back down, putting my arm around her shoulder and pulling her close. "I'm having a good time, sweetheart," I whisper in her ear, her delectable perfume weaving its magic around me once again.

"I am too, Braxton. I wonder how Nan is faring?"

"Let me send her a text," I reply, pulling out my phone. My heart rate increases when I see I've got a text from Mom already, but when I open it, I burst into laughter. "Thinking all is well, y'all," I say, turning the phone around so they can see the picture. Mom set the kids up in the family room apparently, and the three kids are passed out on the pallet on the floor. The caption says, "Wore them slap out, now time for some wine!" Seeing the innocent faces, limbs all over the place, as they sleep has a warmth spreading through my chest. If things were different right now, I'd be booking a room for myself and Cara so I could see *her* limbs spread out as she lay sleeping, sated and satisfied. *Soon.*

"Aw, look at them," Cara says, her finger tracing their little faces while a smile plays on her lips. "They look like they've had fun."

"Knowing Mom, they undoubtedly did," I tell her, sending a quick text back to Mom and then putting my phone away.

"So what do they have available for dessert?" DJ asks. "All that dancing has worked up another appetite."

"Yeah," Hatchet's eyes open wide and I know something tasteless is fixing to come out of his mouth. Therefore, I reach over and grab the menu and hand it to her. "They've got some finger items as well," I state. "I know we ate a full dinner, but

146

I'm good with ordering one of the sampler plates and a few desserts."

"Anything chocolate?" Cara asks.

"They've got a chocolate thunder cake that has vanilla ice cream in the middle covered with hot fudge," I reply. Her face is a little flushed and I don't know if it's from the dancing or the alcohol, but she doesn't strike me as someone who overindulges, so I chalk it up to the dancing.

"That sounds wonderful, can we get one?" she questions.

"Anything you want, sweetheart."

I see a teasing glint come to her eyes before she leans closer and whispers, "Anything?" Her words are a straight shot to my dick and I have to work hard to stifle my groan.

Deciding to tease back, I reply, "Whatever I've got is yours, sweetheart." A tiny whimper escapes and I grin, knowing that my words hit their mark.

Motioning to the waitress, I put in an order for Cara's dessert, refills on the drinks and an appetizer sampler. Hatch, after whispering with DJ, asks for a different dessert and another appetizer. Looks like we're staying for a bit longer.

"Let's dance," I say, holding my hand out to Cara.

Caraleigh

I'm lost in thought trying to remember the last time I had so much fun. Our night finally winds down and I get the impression if we had been alone, I would have broken the longest-running dry spell in the history of dry spells. We leave The Barnhouse and I notice it's around eleven and now we are headed back home. I can't hear the conversation from the back, but I know that DJ and Hatch have really hit it off. Sighing because I know I probably won't get the kisses I'd like, I turn and quietly say, "I really had a good time tonight." I'm starting to feel like a broken record repeating the same thing to him over and over again, I just can't seem to help myself.

"I did too, sweetheart," he replies, turning to grin at me. He's been holding my hand since we got in the truck and the slow, subtle way he's been rubbing my hand has me thinking things that I've never entertained in my life!

I also get the feeling that if DJ and Hatch were alone, they'd be a lot more active than they have been. So this double date may end up being a double-edged sword. Out of the corner of my eye, I see Hatch communicate something to Braxton, using nods and what-not, and my curiosity is roused. "We're making a stop at the clubhouse," Braxton says, interrupting my thoughts.

"We are?"

"Yeah, Hatch and DJ want to have a few more drinks. Do you want to stay or head on home?"

I just want to be alone with him. "Home, I guess, if that's okay with you?"

He grins and says, "Perfectly fine with me."

Once we've dropped Hatch and DJ off, he heads back to the complex, my hand tucked securely in his. Instead of parking in front of my place, he pulls in at his and once he helps me out, says, "Thought I'd walk you home if that's okay?"

As if I'm gonna say no! "That's fine. Would, would you, umm...would you like to come in for a little while?" I rush out before I lose what little nerve I've summoned up.

Braxton

Would I like to come in? Hell yeah I would. I'd like to come in and never leave, but I'm not sure that she's ready for that quite yet. Some alone time with Cara though, has all kinds of racy thoughts in my head. *I wonder if she'd like to do a little making out while we're all alone for the evening?* As those thoughts enter my head, she opens the door and

149

suddenly I'm as nervous as a teenage boy seeing a boob for the first time. Those are the kind of feelings that let me know this is real, this isn't some infatuation that will leave once the sun rises in the morning. Now, I need to climb over those walls and tear them down from the inside out that she's built around herself. I understand why she's built them up, but I don't want them anywhere around when I'm with her. We walk in and she shuts the door behind us, she sets down her keys and purse on a table in the entryway, she leads me to the couch and sits down so I sit next to her.

"I don't have any beer stocked in the fridge, but I do have bottled water and some lemonade made. Would you like anything to drink?"

"Just some water would be good, sweetheart," I tell her. Watching her walk away, I can't help but admire the view in front of me. She is so beautiful, a goddess in her own right. My dick grows hard in my pants, not for the first time tonight. My poor appendage is going to fall off if we keep it up at this rate. I watch as she bends in the fridge and grabs a couple of bottles of water, I am mesmerized by her body. Each graceful movement, every blushing glance—it all has me wanting her. Under me. Over me. Beside me. Something that needs to happen sooner rather than later. I know that it may be too soon for this, but I need her—I need to show her physically and emotionally what she has come to mean to me.

I know a lot of people would condemn me for moving so quickly, but there is something between us that is immovable, it's solid. I'm ready for the day that I can make this delectable woman my old lady—my wife. I want to see her round with with my children. I want her standing next to me, I want to have nightly conversations about our day each night as we lay in bed wound in each other's arms. I want to be a father-figure for Luca, I want to be the man he looks up to and comes to when he has troubles. I want them to trust me, to know that I will always have their backs, and never let them down. They will never need or want for anything as long as I'm around.

"What has you lost in thought over here?" Cara asks me. So I tell her, I tell her everything that was just running through my mind. I look at her the entire time I'm relaying this information and watch as tears run down her cheeks, I know that they're happy tears because she has that smile on her face—the one that lights up the room as you walk in. She sets the waters down on the coffee table and bends over me. I pull her into my lap where she initiates the first kiss, a kiss that means everything to me. A kiss that tells me she's as into this relationship as I am, one that is the beginning of the rest of my life. A new beginning, a brighter future than one I'd ever planned on. "And you don't think we're moving too fast?" she asks once we break apart, breathless.

151

Caressing her back, I reply, "Not at all. Life's too damn short, sweetheart, and neither of us are teenagers who don't know how it works. We've both been hurt and we know what we do and don't want. What I need to know is are you with me? Are you ready to begin the rest of our lives, together? I want this, I want us—forever."

"I'm willing to give this a try, as long as you're aware that if we do this, it's only you for me and me for you."

"There is no trying, sweetheart, when we do this, *and we will*, there is no turning back. You'll be mine forever, you and Luca both."

"It means everything to me that you want my son too, Braxton, and I'm letting you know that the same applies with me. I want you, Lily and Nan."

"Family sweetheart, we'll be a family until each one of us take our last breath."

"That sounds amazing...can we start now?"

"You want me, baby? Do you need me as much as I need you?" Her breathless yes is all I need to hear. I take her by the hand and lead her to her room. Closing and locking the door, I'm grateful that Mom took Lily, Luca and Ralynn overnight so we won't have little ones interrupting. Hell, at this point, I'm glad that Hatch and DJ are staying at the clubhouse! Turning her, I cup her face as I pull her closer, capturing her lips with mine. Long moments pass as I take ownership of her mouth and hearing her moans has me pulling back with a groan of my own.

"Caraleigh, I hope you're ready for what all this means," I murmur as I slowly start undressing her. "Once we do this, there's never going to be a night that you'll be alone as long as I draw breath." Once she's undressed, I lay her down on the bed and gaze at the absolute beauty before me. Face tinged pink, I see my shy woman trying to cover up.

"No, don't cover yourself," I tell her. "This...all of this is mine and I want to see you."

"Braxton, really? I... I mean, *look* at me! I've got stretch marks, a pooch, and my breasts are starting to sag!"

As my eyes trace down her body, I follow with my hands and lips, stopping at each of the areas she has mentioned. Cupping both breasts, I start nuzzling and licking them while my fingers lightly graze over the nipples until they are taut and begging to be sucked. "These right here? They've nourished a child, Cara, and they are perfect," I whisper before taking a nipple into my mouth. After laving one with my tongue and lips, I switch sides while continuing to manipulate the other with my hand.

Stroking the 'stretch marks' that are little more than silvery lines where she once carried Luca and will, someday, carry our children, I lean down and trace each one with my tongue. "And these right here? Are beautiful to me because they show where

153

your delectable body stretched to carry him." She's now writhing a little on the bed and I smile. "They're nothing but roadmaps that show how strong you are for bringing life into this world."

With my face buried in her lower abdomen where, God willing, she'll nurture our future children, I murmur as I lightly nip the skin, "What you see as imperfections is what I see as a place of wonder and joy. I look forward to seeing this stretch when you carry our future sons or daughters."

I can tell she's now out of her negative headspace so I let my fingers and hands do the walking as I spread her thighs, settling my shoulders in between. As I inhale her scent, I hear her whisper, "Braxton," as she slightly twists her hips, begging silently for my mouth to bring her pleasure.

"Beautiful, my gorgeous minx, absolutely breathtaking," I utter before my tongue stretches out and I taste her for the first time. Her taste is addicting, I want to stay here, where I am now, and enjoy the flavors bursting on my tongue.

"Braxton! No...no, we...I mean, you can't do that," she exclaims as she tries-and fails-to close her thighs.

Lifting my head, I look at her and say, "Why?"

"Because I... that...no one has *ever* done that to me!"

What kind of fucking douchebag was her dickhead husband? Realizing that we need to have a

154

conversation before I get where I want to be, I sit back and pull her toward me. Without another word, I scoop her up and sit in the recliner she has in the corner. Once I have her situated on my lap, I turn her head so we are looking at one another.

"What are you doing?" she asks.

"We need to have a conversation and I'll be damned if his ghost will be between us in our bed," I growl out. "Caraleigh, based on all your reactions, I gotta ask, when was the last time you were intimate with him?"

I can feel her shudder before she sighs. "Really? We're talking about this? Now?"

"Yup. So start talking. I want it all, baby, and then? We're making new memories. Ones that will last for all eternity. What did you mean no one has ever gone down on you?"

I watch the blush creep up her face as she closes her eyes and gets her thoughts together. When she starts talking, my mind goes white-hot with rage and I have to work to keep from stiffening up. This beautiful woman will never feel like she can't talk to me. About anything.

"Graham was my first and only lover. I know I've told you things weren't good for a long time before he passed, and I'm the reason."

How in the ever-*loving*-fuck is that possible?

"What do you mean, you were the reason?"

"I... I'm frigid," she whispers.

I can't help it, I start laughing. "Baby, you're so far from frigid it's not funny, but that still doesn't explain what you're trying to tell me." I know she isn't frigid, I know this because of the way her body reacts to me when I touch her. Her body lights up, and I can feel the fire that's inside of her.

She huffs out a breath in frustration, which has me smiling because I know her sass is in there somewhere, before she continues. "I tried to like it but he never took any time with me and I was so inexperienced, I didn't know how to make things better. I mean, I read a lot and all the books I read, the women love it, but me? It wasn't much to write home about, y'know? But to answer your question, I... I haven't had sex since Luca was born."

"How in the hell is that possible?" What man could have this woman as his own and go years without touching her? There is no way I could go hours—days, let alone years, without feeling her writhe under my fingers and my body. Hell, I'm already bemoaning the times when she's got her period for fuck's sake!

"The day I went into labor, he had been out with some work buddies celebrating something or other. I didn't go because it was too far away and I wasn't feeling well. I fell asleep waiting for him to get home and when he finally stumbled in, he was three sheets to the wind. He decided he wanted to 'exercise his husbandly rights' and after it was all over, he passed out. I got up to clean myself up and saw I was bleeding. When I couldn't wake him up, I called my brother who took me to the hospital—where I had Luca eight hours later."

My mind is blank. It sounds like she is saying that he pretty much forced himself on her. "He raped you?" I'm horrified and want to dig his cold body from the ground and beat the living shit out of him!

"It wasn't rape, we were married," she tells me.

"Honey, were you interested? Did you say no?"

"No, I didn't want to have sex," she whispers, her voice so low I barely understand her. "It had been a hard pregnancy and I had been sick that day, so the last thing I wanted was that."

"Then it was rape. Did what he do cause you to go into labor?" I ask. Dammit, the bastard's dead already but my brain is in a consistent loop of 'he must die'...what has this woman done to me? I've never needed to feel blood on my hands like I do at this moment.

She nods. "Luca was two months early," she finally whispers.

Deep breaths. In and out. Again and again until I can feel myself calming. Cuddling her closer, I say, "Cara, I want to say this only once, okay? Your dead husband was a douchebag, plain and simple. If you were inexperienced, it was *his* job as your man to make sure you were comfortable with what was happening and if one position didn't work, keep trying until you were satisfied. The fact that he did

157

that to you without your consent, married or not, was rape plain and simple and I'm sorry you endured that but you will never ever have to worry about that with us. I adore you and this part of our lives will be the best that we can make it. Together. D'you get me, sweetheart?"

She turns to look at me instead of over my shoulder and nods. "I... I really don't know what to do, Braxton, and that makes me nervous. What if I'm not good at it? What if I don't satisfy you? I can't handle losing you from my life. Not now that I finally feel happy for the first time in a long time. You've come to mean more to me than my next intake of breath."

Alright, conversation's over. I stand, lifting her in my arms and carry her back over to the bed, gently laying her down before I strip out of my own clothes. Climbing in next to her, I curl her so we are face-to-face and say, "As far as before me—us, that was then and this is now. I have absolutely no doubt that we will burn with each other's touch, y'hear? And I'm quite confident that we'll *both* be satisfied. Now, kiss me," I demand, needing to feel her lips upon mine.

She leans forward to kiss me and I can tell when she realizes that I'm hard because her face once again turns pink. Taking her hand, I move it to my dick and hear her little gasp of breath before she takes hold. Compared to mine, her hand looks so small, but the way she's gripping me has me moaning as I deepen the kiss, threading my fingers through her hair to pull her closer.

"Like your hand on me, my Cara," I whisper.

"Like it a helluva lot."

"You...you're so big, Braxton, I don't think it's going to fit."

Genuine mirth at her statement has me laughing out loud. "Ah, my sweet innocent Cara, I'm going to fit. I have no doubt we were made for each other."

"I'm not innocent, Braxton, I've had a child!"

Running my nose alongside hers, I say, "When it comes to this, you are, sweetheart." And I can't wait to show her—to teach her all the ways we will work, and fit together.

"Oh."

"Yeah, 'oh'." Deciding that I'm tired of talking when we should be doing other things, I begin kissing her neck while my hand roams down to her breast where I squeeze and manipulate it before lowering my head and taking the nipple into my mouth. As I continue my assault, she starts moving restlessly. *You ain't seen nothing yet, babe.* I had a small taste of her and plan to go back.

Moving down the bed, I spread her legs and look, seeing the evidence of her desire glistening between the folds of the prettiest pussy I've ever seen. Leaning closer, I take her clit into my mouth and use my lips and tongue to increase her passion. The second taste was as good as the first and I give

159

in to it, settling my shoulders so that her legs now rest down my back. Glancing up, I see her head thrown back and her hands clutching at the sheets as she moves restlessly.

"Oh my God, Braxton, it feels so...oh shit—so good," she whimpers. It isn't often that I've heard a curse word leave her luscious mouth, knowing that I have this affect on her drives me to hear more.

"Gonna make you come so hard for me, beautiful, want you coming on my tongue and fingers," I say before diving back in as if I'm the fat kid at the buffet. Easing a single finger inside, I can feel how hot and tight she is, and I want to groan out loud at how it's going to feel once I have my dick sheathed in the warmth and tight—ness of her pussy. Lightly stroking her clit with my thumb, I ease a second finger inside, all while continuing my ministrations with my lips and tongue. Her taste is fucking addictive and I vow that I will never—ever give this up.

I feel her body tensing and I can sense how close she is. "Give it to me, Cara, I want it. No keeping it buried inside, sweetheart, don't ever hold yourself back from me. I need to feel youhear you. Scream out your release, call out my name when you come."

With a muffled groan, her orgasm rolls through her and I continue lapping at her until her shudders slow. She screams out my name as I requested and I feel like I've defeated the reigning heavyweight

160

champion. And all his cohorts. Knowing she's overly sensitized, I give her clit one last lick before I move over her body, dropping small sensual kisses along the way as I go. When I'm fully laying over the top of her with my dick nestled between her legs, I cup her face and say, "Gonna make you mine now, beautiful."

"Mmmm," she moans. "That was phenomenal." As I slowly enter her, I see her eyes widen before she sighs a little and spreads her legs further. Holy fucking hell—she's as tight as a vise and if I'm not careful, I'll end up being a two-pump chump.

"So tight, so wet, so hot...so mine," I whisper in her ear. Once I'm fully seated inside, I lean my forehead against hers and ask, "You good, Cara?"

"Braxton," she breathes out, "I feel so...so full."

Chuckling lightly, I begin moving—slowly. I'm willing to bet that my woman has never come before with anyone, other than herself—and now? Now I want her coming on my dick. "Caraleigh, want you to come on my dick," I tell her, my hips picking up speed. I go from slow and sensual to a mad man needing to feel her squeeze me with her tightness.

"I... I don't know if I can," she whimpers. Based on how she just came on my tongue and fingers and the fact that I can feel her pussy beginning to tighten on my dick, I'm convinced my earlier assessment is correct—she never got off before. Well, that will never again be an issue for her.

As my pace increases, I reach down and lightly tap her leg, saying, "Wrap these long, luscious legs around me, Cara," then nearly groan out loud when she does and I sink deeper inside of her delicious body. I know I'm not going to last much longer so I reach between us and pinch her clit then I start to lightly stroke her, hoping to help her reach her pleasure quicker.

"Braxton!" she screams as she comes undone in my arms, her pussy milking my dick so hard that it forces my orgasm out of me as well. Hearing her scream my name again pushes me to go deeper and quicken my pace even more.

Leaning in, I capture her lips in mine as I begin to slow my thrusts while she rides her orgasm out. Finally reaching nirvana myself, I am breathless, so I lean over and rest my forehead on hers. "You okay, sweetheart?"

Shining eyes look at me and she says, "I never knew it could be like this. Hell yes, I'm good. I'm fantastic even. When can we do that again?"

Laughter bursts forth and I look at her before nipping her earlobe. "Give me a few and we'll be good to go, yeah?" I think I might have created a nympho and I couldn't be any prouder or happier. I can tell she's going to keep me on my toes...and I can't wait.

CHAPTER NINE

Braxton

Monday comes too quickly, and the next thing I know, I'm sitting in chapel with my brothers and church is taking place. There are ten of us patched members so far, but we have four prospects who are working their asses off to become brothers. I know our club is smaller than most which is why we've hired outside the MC for the trucking company. I shake my head thinking of the current receptionist. Starla has made no bones about the fact that she likes Hatchet, but she's been flirting unmercifully with me in an effort to make him jealous. Don't think my woman is going to go for that at all. We're doing the boring part at the moment, going over the financials, and setting up the trucking company runs for the next week. I'm finding myself lost in thoughts of Caraleigh and the way she felt in my arms as we laid in bed after a night filled with making love.

"Earth to Axe," Twisted calls out. I didn't even realize anyone had been speaking to me.

"Sorry guys, lost in my head there. What did I miss?"

"Depends, how long were you in la-la land?" Hatchet asks with a smirk on his face, one I'd love nothing more than to wipe away. With my fist to his face, though DJ may not forgive me if I rearrange his appearance any.

"Keep it up, Hatch, and you and I will have a personal meeting in the parking lot," I growl out in frustration.

"Just because you're sexually frustrated doesn't mean you gotta take it out on the rest of us," he says. If only he knew. Guessing my girl hasn't shared with hers just yet and that makes me smile, knowing that is ours and ours alone—for the time being anyways. If anything, I'm waiting for DJ and Paisley to pull it out of her, they're some nosey ass bitches.

"So, to recap for you since you weren't listening, you've got the run to Cali this week with those parts, Hatch is taking the one to the East Coast, and I'll keep shit running here," Twisted says, breaking into my thoughts. "We're all good with you making Cara your old lady, thinking she'll be a good fit, brother. And she's starting tomorrow at the trucking company. You'll leave once you get her squared away, okay?"

I nod my head. Hate that I'll be gone after the night—and morning—that we shared, but she knows we're trying to get more drivers and until then, I'm on the runs. She did mention that she was going to contact the local technical college that had a CDL program to see if they had any recent graduates they could recommend. I like that idea and decide I need to mention it while we're all here in the same place. "Cara is going to call the tech college, y'all, and see if they have any recent graduates that are looking for a job."

"Think that's a good idea," Chief says. "You need to be here more so you can be with your daughter. I understand why you've been taking the runs, but she needs you too." I happen to agree with his assessment, only it's not only Lily that I need to be home for anymore. Needing to change the subject and get it off me I ask if there's any other business that needs to be brought up at today's meeting.

"What about your mom and her shenanigans here at the clubhouse?" Hatchet asks me. I'm glad he brought it up, I was so focused on getting the attention off of myself that I completely forgot that she's taken over here.

"I'm seriously debating taking her credit cards and keys away from her," I say with all seriousness.

"Sure, then we all get to hand over cash when she needs it and we start a driving service. We'll be driving miss daisy!"

"The fact that you even know about that movie, Hatchet, is a bit disturbing," I say to him.

"What? I like Morgan Freeman," he says, which has the rest of us laughing.

165

"Alright, we know what we want done around here, maybe we let her know that before she embarks on her next trip to Ikea, she has to tell us so we're prepared," I state. "That way, if we're not ready for something, we can hold her off."

"Yeah, like a stampede of wildebeasts," Hatch states, causing more laughter around the room.

"It's a better solution than each one of us being her keeper," I say with my eyebrows raised at my brothers.

"She's very persistent," Chief mutters. "I was concerned the day she tried to get in here, considering this is our sanctuary away from the women...period."

"I agree, this room is sacred to the brothers, everything done and said in here is confidential and patched club members are the only ones allowed to enter those doors. It's in our bylaws," Twisted says with a voice of finality. They're right, this room is off-limits to anyone not wearing a bottom rocker on their cut.

"Alright, guys, I'll deal with Mom later and make the stipulations known to her of what she is and isn't allowed to do without our approval first. Any other business?" No one says anything and I see a lot of head shakes. "This meeting is adjourned," I slam down my gavel indicating that everyone can leave. As the brothers get up and leave the room, I stay in my chair and am thinking of how disappointed I am in the fact that I'll be leaving so soon.

"You alright, man?" Twisted asks me, I wasn't aware that he'd stuck around. I need to get better about being lost in my thoughts and not be one-hundred percent aware of my surroundings.

"I'm good, brother, just thinking about life and how quickly it can change."

"What's with the frown then? I thought all the changes happening with you are what you want."

"They are, just wishing I wasn't leaving so quick after making Cara mine is all. I don't even think at this point an overnight trip would be welcoming to me...you get my drift?"

"I getcha, man, I don't think I could personally take being away from Paisley and Tig for even a short amount of time either." Which I know is a fact, he told me once he married her and their son was born that he'd no longer be taking any runs, he wanted to stay in the background and run things from our office. He'll sometimes take a day run, as long as he's home in time for dinner, he gives me no shit. He likes handling the office things that drive me insane, so it's a win-win situation as far as I was concerned in the beginning. Things have changed however, and I want nothing more than to sit behind a desk beside him so I'm home every night as well. "Don't worry Axe, I've got your back, I'll help Cara get us more drivers so you can stay home more often." He slaps me on the back, stands up and walks out of the room with determination marked on his face. My brothers, they always take care of me, even when I don't realize I need it.

Knowing I need to get home and take my baby girl to dinner, I shoot Cara a text message.

Braxton: Would you and Luca like to go to dinner with Lily and me?
Cara: Yes
Braxton: Be there soon sweetheart
Cara: Can't wait...I've missed you today. I am excited to see you
Braxton: Same here, beautiful, I missed holding you in my arms. See ya soon

I put my phone in my back pocket and get on my bike, damn it's good to be me. With a smile on my face I head towards the house to grab my family and treat them to a night out.

Caraleigh

This day has dragged on, DJ didn't get home until after Braxton had left this morning. When she got home, she had a cup of coffee and I had some lemonade. We talked about our double-date last

168

night, but we didn't get into what happened once we went our separate ways. I'm kind of glad about that, though, because I'm still processing everything he said and all that we did. Once we felt like we had enough energy stored, we went down to Braxton's and picked up our two rugrats, who were anything but pleased to be leaving Lily's side. Back at home, we downloaded an enrollment packet and got it filled out so that things would be easier for DJ when she goes in the morning to enroll Ralynn in school. This morning as we were talking, we decided that while DJ went home to pack up her house and settle a few things, I would keep Ralynn so she could go ahead and start at the school with the other kids.

We printed out Ralynn's transcripts from her homeschooling hoping to make things simpler, and easier for her to begin right away. Luca talks to Ralynn throughout the day about his new school and how much fun it is. I see the weight leave her shoulders, poor girl is a ball of nerves at going to a school with kids in it. She's so used to doing things in her own time frame, and it just being her mother and her, that she managed to work herself up.

"You're going to have so much fun going to the same school as Luca and Lily," I say to her, trying to encourage her and get her excited. "Who knows, you may all have lunch and recess together."

"I hopes so," she says to me, blowing her bangs out of her eyes.

"Yous will loves it, Ray," Luca tells her.

169

"Oh, honey bear, think of it this way, you won't be lonely anymore," DJ reminds her.

"That's trues," she says nodding her head up and down. At the rate she's moving I'm worried she's going to shake her head off the top of her shoulders. I hear my phone ping with a notification from my pocket. I pull my phone out and notice a text from Braxton. I smile at him asking me and Luca out for dinner. I look at the time and see it's already five p.m. Time really flew today once we got the kids. We send a couple of texts back and forth and excitement bubbles inside my stomach.

"Hey Luca, Braxton has invited you and me to dinner with him and Lily, you want to go?"

"Yes, yes, yes! But whats about Ray? Is she coming too?" I look at DJ, I'm a sorry excuse for a friend, I didn't even think about her or Ralynn.

"Oh, I forgot to tell you. I told Hatchet that Ralynn and I would go to dinner with him tonight, then we're taking Ralynn to buy some new school supplies and clothes. He suggested she may want some new things to start school with. I thought it was a sweet idea and couldn't say no when he asked me."

"Awww, that was so thoughtful of him. I have a feeling though that it is just an excuse to spend more time with you and get Ralynn on his side," I say batting my eyelashes at her. We've always teased each other, and this time is no exception to that rule.

170

"He doesn't need an excuse," I hear her say under her breath.

"What was that?" I ask, even though I heard her perfectly fine.

"Nothing, it was nothing. We printed up the school supply list for her grade, do you have any other suggestions on things she'll need?" she asks, changing the subject. She must really like Hatchet not to come back with a sarcastic remark...so unlike my friend.

"There isn't a dress code at the school so I can't think of anything else to add."

"Don't forgets, she'll need a pillow and blanket for nap time. Lily has her own and so do all the others," Luca informs us. He doesn't have nap time, so those items never even came to mind.

"Good idea, buddy."

"Thanks yous." I can't help but smile at his thoughtfulness.

"You're a good friend, Luca, I'm going to add that to her list right now." DJ praises him, which causes him to puff his chest out under her praise. Forty-five minutes later, there's a knock at the door, instantly knowing who it is I rush over and fling the door open in excitement.

"Jesus, woman, you didn't even ask who it was, did you even look out the peephole?"

"Calm down, Braxton, I knew it was you?"

"You did, huh? And how exactly did you know that?" Good question, I've got nothing.

171

"Exactly, there's precious cargo in this house. Don't ever do that again…. please," he adds at the end, smoothing out his aggressive demeanor.

"I promise, I'll be more careful in the future."

"Thank you, that's all I can ask, now—get those lips over here and welcome me properly." I do as asked until we hear three kids all saying, "ewww!" Which causes the three adults in the room to break out into laughter.

"Does this mean you're my momma's boyfriend?" Luca asks Braxton, causing me to freeze instantly. This is something we didn't talk about, how we were going to tell the kids about us.

Braxton kneels down in front of Luca, "I was hoping to talk to you about this, as the man in her life. Would it be okay with you if I was? I would like very much to be, I really care about you and your mom, Luca."

"Does that mean you'd be my new daddy too?" he asks apprehensively.

"I don't know about all of that, you had a daddy, until we decide, you and I, about it, I'd really like to be your friend. Can we do that first and then we'll talk about the other later?"

"Okays, I'm starvlin, can we go to dinner now?"

"Me too," Lily puts her two-cents in. Knowing that this topic is officially closed so easily takes weight off my chest. I need to talk to Braxton and see how he feels about my son's slight inquisition.

172

"We're off, Hatchet texted me a few minutes ago and told me he was on his way to pick you and Ralynn up, so I guess we don't need to bring you back dinner?" Braxton asks DJ.

"No we're good, you guys have fun and we'll see you later." With that, Braxton grabs my hand and we're out the door.

Dinner was fun, we took the kids to a local hamburger diner, where they had milkshakes and we played some games with them in the kids playground area. It was a good idea for them to build a play area for kids, the place was packed! It became overwhelming so we left, and we stopped at the park because the kids still had a lot of built up energy. I stood wrapped in Baxton's arms as the kids slid down the slide, played on the merry go round and pushed each other on the swings. Now we're home and I don't want to let him go, I know I'll see him early in the morning, but it doesn't make it any easier to tell him goodnight. We drop Lily off with Nan and Braxton walks Luca and I home. It's a bittersweet feeling to be home, on one hand I'm exhausted, on another I want to take Braxton to my room and have some fun once Luca's asleep.

Knowing he needs to spend some time with Lily, I send Luca to his room so Braxton can wish me goodbye properly. Standing in my living room, both of our hands intertwined, he leans down and places a slow gentle kiss to my lips. He swipes his tongue across and I open immediately giving him access to insert his tongue into my mouth. I moan into his mouth, we kiss for a few minutes before he pulls away.

"I don't want to leave, but I promised Lily I'd give her a bath and read her a story before bed. Some cat story she's reading at school. She brought the book home and has been begging me to read it to her. I've gotta go, baby," I melt at him calling me baby.

"I know," I tell him breathlessly. We untangle our hands and I walk him over to the door, once inside the door frame, he kisses me again.

"Lock this behind me," he says and steps back allowing me to shut the door. I lean my forehead against it trying to get control of my emotions. "Lock the door, Cara." Shit, I didn't realize he was standing outside the door listening for when the lock engaged!

I lock the door and holler out, "Okay, bossy! The damn door is locked, go home to your daughter." I hear him chuckle before he calls out one final goodnight to me.

Making my way upstairs, I walk into Luca's room to see him playing with his dinosaurs. He's on his bed and when he notices I entered his room he says to me, "Momma, I really likes Mr. Braxton, I wouldn't minds him beins my new daddy." I'm lost for words at what I should say to him, Braxton and I really need to have a conversation about all of this.

"Sweetie, I'm glad you like him. I like him a lot too." Smooth, Cara, now how about addressing what *else* he said? The elephant that is in this room is weighing heavily upon my shoulders. "I don't think we're at that point yet, but I'm glad you would be okay if he and I got married someday. You know that if that were to ever happen, he wouldn't replace your daddy, right?"

"Of courses him wouldn't, Momma! But my daddy is in Heavens now and I is going to needs a daddy to learn to be a big, strong man. Uncle Chan teached me a lot, but him doesn't lives here."

My heart is overfull right now at my son's words and I am absolutely speechless. "Luca, you're such a good boy and you're already growing up to be a fine young man."

He's apparently done with our heart-to-heart, because his next words have me laughing. "Momma, can we sees if we has any ice cream? My tummy has a hole in it."

"Come on, I think we can handle that and then? Let's get your bath out of the way so when Ralynn and DJ get home, she can take hers. Do you want to surprise her and make her sandwich for her lunch?"

"We need cookies, too!" he tells me as he goes to rush downstairs. Calling out his name, I see him stop, take a breath and then walk down the stairs. Always in such a hurry to get from point A to point B, *one day I'm not going to be there to remind him to slow down.*

By the time he has eaten his ice cream and made two peanut butter and fluffernutter sandwiches, I have the cookie dough made. "Okay, young man, head upstairs and get your bath started."

"I can't makes the cookies?"

Looking at the clock, I see it's later than normal so I shake my head no. "I'll make sure they're all done once you go to bed and you two can pack them in your lunchboxes in the morning, okay?"

He sighs and I have to hold back my smile. "Okays, Momma."

I get his water started then head into his room to gather his pajamas. "Let's go ahead and pick out your clothes for tomorrow."

Running in, he pulls out a yellow t-shirt with some game character on it and says, "This one!"

"Who is that?" I ask, looking at the crazy blue creature.

"Momma! It's Sonic!" As if that tells me anything! Deciding I won't show my ignorance because I'm supposed to know everything, I merely nod then point toward the bedroom door, grabbing his book as I follow him.

"We're running late tonight, buddy, so I'm going to read to you while you wash up, okay?"

Thirty minutes later, bath done, teeth brushed and one very tired little boy tucked in, I head into my room to figure out what I'm wearing for my first day at work. I don't really have anything that would be considered office wear, but he said it didn't matter, so I find my favorite pair of jeans and a flowy, off the shoulder, top. I'll pair it with my boots, I guess. "That looks good," DJ's voice says, causing me to jump.

"Shit! I didn't even hear y'all come back!" I tell her, my heart pounding a mile a minute.

She bursts into laughter, making me want to hit her. "Yeah, already got Ray in the tub, just wanted to see what you were doing."

"Well, now that I'm done with this, I'll be headed down to make cookies. Luca felt it would be a nice addition to their lunches."

"She'll love that, you want some help? She's already passed out and I have to wash some of the things we bought tonight."

"Let's get this done, shall we?" I ask.

Braxton

"Daddy?" Lily's voice pulls me from my thoughts. "Is Miss Cara going to be my mommy?"

Eventually, yes. Yes, she is. Nope, can't tell her that yet, especially since Cara doesn't know. "We just started dating, sweet pea, so it's a little early for that, don't you think?"

"She'd make a good mommy, I want her to be my mommy and Luca to bes my brother," she murmurs. We'd done the bath and jammies and I had just finished reading to her now that she's tucked in bed. Her sleepy voice makes me realize that she's almost out, so instead of responding, I lean over and smooth away her hair and kiss her.

"Good night, sweet pea. I'll see you in the morning bright and early, okay?"

"M'kay, Daddy. I loves you," she mumbles, turning toward the wall, her doll tucked under her arm.

"Love you too."

Back downstairs, I'm feeling at loose ends. I would love nothing more than to walk a few doors down, knock, then carry a certain female upstairs to make love to her all night long. Yeah, not happening tonight. Dammit. I grab a beer and sit down with the remote to see what I can find to watch.

"Braxton?" Hearing Mom, I turn the volume down and motion for her to continue. "How was your night out?"

178

Yeah, like I'm gonna tell my mom how it went. Nope, not going there. "Had a good time, Mom. What's up?"

"You've got a trip this week?"

"Yeah, out to Cali to deliver some parts. Just making sure Cara knows the lay of the land at the office before I head out."

"I really like her."

"Yeah, me too. You good for money while I'm gone?"

She gives me an offended look before saying, "You should know better than that by now. We're fully stocked up and don't forget, I have my own accounts."

"That you shouldn't have to spend from, Mom. You're taking care of my house and Lily, remember?" I shake my head at her stubbornness.

"Braxton, I have more money saved up than I'll use in my lifetime!"

"Considering you're living until you're as old as Methusalah, that's a good thing, Mom." A throw pillow comes flying at me and I duck. "Really? Kind of childish, isn't it?"

She gets up and tosses a "good night" over her shoulder. Great, now she's pissed at me. May as well head on up to bed, it's going to be a long week. I check the doors and windows, one of those long-standing habits, then make my way upstairs. One more peek in at Lily has me straightening her out on her bed and retucking the blankets around her tiny form.

Caraleigh

The next morning finds me running around like a chicken with my head cut off. Both kids are a bit grumpy because of their fun-filled weekend with late nights and no schedule and I've reached my limit when Luca whines. "Luca! I said enough! Finish your breakfast and then go and brush your teeth. Now!"

Ralynn, who was also a bit whiny, starts shoveling her cereal in without speaking. Guess it pays to occasionally crack the whip, huh?

"Uh-oh, looks like you two are misbehaving this morning," DJ says, coming in and going directly over to the coffee pot. "Considering how much fun you both had this past weekend, seems to me you wouldn't want to start the week getting into trouble. Now, what's the problem, Ray?"

Leave it to DJ to get to the nuts and bolts. Me? I'm just what my mom would call outdone. Getting both of them up and dressed was like pulling hen's teeth, and then? They bickered over which cereal they were going to eat, which seat they were going to sit at, even which juice glass they wanted to use!

Sipping my diet soda, I give her a look to convey it was "everything".

"Ray? I'm waiting," she states, stirring in some sugar. "And seeing as you both still have to brush your teeth then we have to head to school? Your time is up."

"Mommy, I'm tired," Ray says. "I don't wanna goes to school today. I didn't want Frosted Flakes and then Luca got the bestest seat."

DJ rolls her eyes at me and I bite back a grin. "Suck it up, buttercup. You are going to school today and as far as what cereal you're eating, you've always enjoyed Frosted Flakes which is why we bought them. And that is Luca's seat, we're guests, remember?"

Ralynn's eyes tear up and her lips wobble. "Ah ah...no tears, missy. If you're both so tired, then I'll let Nan know that you need a nap after she picks you up from school. How does that sound?"

"No! Not a nap!" they both cry out.

"Then what do you suggest?"

They fall over themselves apologizing, words coming out of their mouths that have me choking back laughter.

"Hmm, that's all well and good that you're both sorry and I'm sure Cara appreciates it, but I think that early bedtime this week might do you both some good so you remember that cranky kids have consequences." Damn, she's good at this shit!

181

"I like your idea, DJ," I state. "Now, you two need to go up and brush your teeth so we can head out. I start my new job today and do not plan to be late."

Ten minutes later, DJ has the two kids in her car and headed toward school while I quickly clean up the kitchen before leaving. I am one of those women—I can't leave dishes hanging until later. I credit my mom for that, she is affectionately known as Mrs. Clean for her housekeeping ways. Guess it bled into me. Grabbing my insulated bag that has a small lunch in it and a few drinks, I head off to work.

"Cara?" Nan calls out as I reach my car.

"Hey, Nan. Thanks again for watching the kids this weekend so we could go out."

"Never a problem, dear. How were the kids this morning?"

"Oh my goodness, we had two brats instead of well-behaved rugrats, that's for sure."

"Yeah, Lily was the same. I know I'm picking them all up today, would it be okay if they had a little rest?"

I can't help it, I start laughing. When I finally calm down, I say, "DJ told them that if they couldn't behave, she was going to make sure you had them take a nap every day! They weren't happy about that at all."

"Well, once I make sure they've done their homework and give them a snack, I'll have them watch a movie or something. No major running around."

"I trust your judgement. We told them they would have early bedtime this week, which they aren't happy with, but DJ reminded them that actions have consequences."

"Yes they do and both kids are so well-behaved, it's obvious that you and DJ are doing something right with them. I know you're headed off to work and it's your first day. With Braxton leaving on his trip, come home planning to eat dinner. Let DJ know as well."

"Nan, we can't ask you to do that, you're already doing so much!" I protest.

"You're not asking, I'm telling you that's what we're going to do, okay? I love cooking and if it helps the two of you, then all the better. In fact, I'll have DJ bring over whatever it is you make for the kids' sandwiches and I'll get the kids to make their lunches as well. That way, once you two get them home and bathed and put to bed, you can relax."

"Nan, you're a lifesaver, that's for sure! It's been so long since I've worked that I was a bit worried, to be honest. Especially once DJ goes back to her house to get things finalized before she moves because then? I'll have two kids to take care of!"

"We'll manage dear. Now, you head off to work, I'm sure you're anxious to see Braxton."

183

A light blush covers my face and I nod. "Are you...are you okay with how fast all of this," I wave my hands in the air, "seems to be happening?"

"Caraleigh, I've never seen my son so happy. Ever. Even being Lily's dad, he has had a cloud of sadness that surrounded him and I've prayed for years that someone like you would come along and light up his world. So no, I don't think it's 'too fast', I think the prayers were finally answered."

At her words, I can't help it, I reach out and give her a hug. She's so fucking different from Mrs. Jensen, my mother-in-law, and I need her to know she's important. "Nan, I think I love you," I whisper.

She chuckles lightly then says, "I already love you and Luca and your crazy friend and her little girl, dear. Now, scoot."

Ah shit, she used the mom tone on me. With a wave, I turn and get into my car. Time to go to work!

Braxton

"I'm sure she'll like the office, Axe," Twisted says as I wipe the top of the desk off. Again. "And don't forget, even though you'll be gone, I'm here

184

and Paisley works out in the warehouse. She'll be fine."

"Kinda worried more about Starla, if you want the truth."

"Starla? Why? She's just the receptionist."

"Who wants Hatch and who has been flirting with me incessantly," I tell him.

"Well, you'll get that straightened out as soon as you ask Cara to be your old lady and she starts wearing your cut."

"True. Fuck, forgot to have Law order it."

"No worries, I took care of it for you."

"This is why you're my VP."

We walk out of the office that Cara's going to use and I see her pulling into the parking lot. "Be right back."

I see her face light up when she spots me and I quickly walk over to her car and open her door once she's shut it off and unlocked them. "Hey, sweetheart." God, I can't get over how beautiful she is, every time I see her I want to ravish her on the spot.

"Hey, Braxton," she replies, a light blush covering her face. I want to pull her into me and kiss her breathless but...we're in the parking lot. Wouldn't be very professional of the boss, especially on her first day, I'm sure she wants to make a good impression with the workers. Regardless, I'm already hard as a rock, and am

185

having a hard time reminding that to a certain appendage of that fact. *Down boy!*

"C'mon, let me show you around and give you the lay of the land." Grabbing her hand, I lead her into the building. "That's where our receptionist, Starla, sits," I say, motioning to the front desk.

Walking down the hall, I bypass my office and Twisted's, until I get to the third door. "Here's your office," I tell her, pulling her in and shutting the door. Before she can say anything, I gently tug her closer until she's in my arms. "Good morning, sweetheart," I whisper before I claim her lips with mine.

We're both breathless by the time I pull back and I grin at the slightly bemused look on her face. Tucking a strand of hair behind her ear, I kiss her nose and say, "I think I'm going to like you being here."

"Braxton! We're...we're at work!"

"And I'm the boss."

She moves to sit behind the desk and I shake my head no. "Just put your purse up, the key to lock the desk is in the top drawer. I want to show you around before you get started, okay?"

"Alright," she replies. She places her purse and another small bag in the bottom drawer and locks it up, putting the key in her front pocket.

As we walk around, I introduce her to the other employees, giving the guys the eye whenever they stray from her face. I want to beat my chest and yell out that she's mine, but she and I have to have that conversation first. So, stern looks will have to do. *For now.*

"Cara!" Paisley calls out, coming from the small warehouse office she works in. "I didn't know you were gonna be working here!"

Cara looks at me and grins. "Yeah, that happened over the weekend."

Paisley looks at the two of us and smiles. I'm trying to be discreet, so I don't have her hand in mine, and I haven't pulled her into my side. But if these fuckers keep eyeballing her? All bets are off.

"Well, glad to have you on board. If you need help with anything, just holler, I've been here since the beginning and have probably done every job."

"What do you do back here?" Cara asks.

"I oversee the warehouse shipments. I'll show you later what I mean, but some of our customers have inventory shipped here, and we keep it stocked for them, so when they need it delivered, we load it up and ship it out."

"I'm glad you're here," she replies. "It'll make it easier having someone I know if Braxton is out on a run."

"No worries, girl, we'll get you up to speed in no time. Braxton, you got a minute?"

I look at Paisley and see she has paperwork in her hand. "Is that what I need?"

"Yeah, just wanted to make sure you knew what to expect. The order is more than last time, so I am having to call and increase our bond. Do you want me to make that a permanent change?"

Blowing out a breath, I nod. "Seems like that would be the way to go, so yes. Definitely get the maximum so we're covered in case anything happens."

"What is she talking about?" Cara asks.

"We've got a bonded and insured warehouse, sweetheart. But sometimes, like with the shipment I'm hauling this week, the cost to replace them could be more than our policy covers in the event of an accident or fire, anything of that nature. She's going to get us the maximum coverage we can get."

"Oh, that makes sense," she replies, looking at the different areas in the warehouse. I see Hatch at one bay door, watching as the forklift driver loads pallet after pallet of dry goods.

"C'mon, there's more to see. We'll catch you later, Paisley."

"Sounds good. Welcome aboard, Cara! We'll definitely do lunch sometime this week, okay?"

Cara nods and I turn her and go back to the office area. "Here's the breakroom, we keep the fridge stocked with what folks enjoy drinking, so if there's something you'd like, let Chef know, he's in charge of that shit. Down here is the conference room. Sometimes, clients want to come in and meet with us and see we're not a bunch of meatheads."

Her laughter catches me off-guard and I look at her. "What's so funny?"

188

"Y'all are so far from that description it's ridiculous. Is it because you're bikers?"

Damn she's gonna make me a great old lady!

"Yeah, sweetheart, it is. But they don't realize that most of the men except the prospects have degrees of one kind or another. Hell, Law is an attorney!"

"Well, see? That just goes to show you can't judge a book by its cover, right?"

"Exactly. Now, let me show you what you'll be doing."

We walk back to her office, passing Starla. "Starla, this is Caraleigh. She's our new office manager."

"Good morning," Cara says.

Starla's eyebrow goes up when she sees how close I am to Cara, but she responds, barely, and says, "Good morning." Twisted is right, I need to keep an eye on her. Making a mental note to speak with Hatch, I nod and keep us moving toward her office.

We've spent the past three hours going over the computer system and what her job duties will be when Twisted walks in. "Hey y'all, thought it would be a good time to break for lunch before you leave, Braxton. What do you think?"

Cara's stomach growls at the mention of food and the three of us laugh. "Guess that's our answer, brother," I reply. "Did you bring her the paperwork for payroll and shit?"

"Yeah, I have it right here," he says, handing her a sheaf of papers. "We need to get you into the computer so you'll get a paycheck. We can do real checks or direct deposit, your choice. I'd recommend the direct deposit because it goes in the day before payday. I think the first one is a live check, but after that, direct deposit."

"Then that's what I'll do. Is Paisley coming to lunch too?"

"Absolutely. She wants Mexican. That alright with you two?"

I nod because I know from talking to her that she enjoys it and the little restaurant around the corner has quick, friendly service.

"Take the bikes?" Twisted asks.

"Absolutely," I tell him. "Cara, you might want to braid your hair."

"Why?"

"So the helmet doesn't mess it up too much."

"Okay. Can you give me ten minutes? I'll get it taken care of."

"We'll meet you out front, okay?"

She nods at me and I resist—barely—the urge to kiss her. Twisted snorts and I give him a death glare. Fucker.

Waiting at the bikes, I see both women coming out the front doors laughing. Cara has managed to put her hair into a French braid and my hands are itching to take it down, see all those curls that I love spread across my pillow. *Get a grip, Braxton, you know it's gonna be harder than hell riding with your dick standing straight up!* I grab the extra helmet I have and help her get it on. "You ever been on the back of a bike, sweetheart?"

She's looking at my bike and biting her lip, Lord have mercy with what I want to do with that lip of hers. I can see the apprehension growing on her face. Dropping a quick kiss on her forehead, I pull her lip from her teeth and straddle my bike. Then I tell her how to get on behind me. Once she's in place, her chest crushed against my back, I hit the ignition and fire up my other girl. "Hold on, sweetheart, don't let your legs touch those pipes," I point showing her which ones I mean, "and when I lean, lean with me, okay?"

I feel her nod behind me as her grip tightens around my waist. I pat her leg and pull out, Twisted next to me with Paisley riding bitch. I hope she falls in love with riding, there's nothing like it and I can envision us taking day trips on the bike. Shit, I can even see some nighttime escapes on my bike, and think about the things we could do while we're out and about. I've found some pretty desolate places, where I could rip off her clothes, and have my wicked way with her while she's leaned over my

191

bike. Yeah, we're definitely going to have to have Mom watch the kids some night—soon.

Caraleigh

Holy fucking shit! I had no clue that the vibrations would be such a turn on for me, but right now? If he were to touch me, I'd go off like fireworks on the Fourth of July. We stop at a light and he hollers back, "You doing okay?" Ummm...how can I answer his question without sounding like an excited minx?

I lean closer, if that's even possible, and say, "Yes. But we gotta talk." He pats my leg again and then takes off when the light turns green. We pull into a Mexican restaurant and he helps me off. "My legs feel a little bit like jello," I confess as he takes my helmet and puts it in the saddlebag next to his.

"That's normal, sweetheart. You'll get used to it. Now what do we have to talk about?"

I lean in closer and pull him down so I'm whispering in his ear. There's no way in hell I want Twisted or Paisley to know my current predicament! "Those vibrations...um...well, hell, no other way but to say it—they turned me on!" Should I tell him I want to do this as much as we possibly can?

His chuckle sends shivers down my spine. "We may have to figure out how we can handle that, sweetheart, especially with me sporting a hard-on." I glance down and can feel the fire hit my cheeks as his jeans show the evidence of his desire.

"But...how? I mean, you're getting ready to leave."

"Sweetheart, I have to go back to the office. And... just saying, my door has a lock and my office is soundproof."

"Won't anyone think something's going on?" I ask as we make our way into the restaurant.

"Nope. Twisted will likely do the same thing with Paisley when we get back."

I know my eyebrows are now in my hairline. I mean, it *is* a place of business and here we are, talking about a quickie! He grins at me and I blush. "C'mon, sweetheart, let's get something to eat." When he says the word eat, he says it in a husky voice, causing me to imagine myself being his menu of choice.

Lunch ends up being a lot of fun and I find myself laughing at the stories that Twisted and Braxton share about starting up the business. Soon, we're back on the bikes heading back to the office and my stomach clenches at what is to come. Both Paisley and I took a few minutes at the restaurant and I freshened up a bit. I blush thinking of the knowing look on her face when she said, "So, looks like things are cooking with gas between you two." All I could do was nod. I know you're supposed to share these things with your girlfriends, but for now, I want to keep this to myself. I don't want to share that part of him with them, or anyone yet.

When we walk back into the building, the receptionist looks up and smiles flirtatiously at Braxton and I find myself gritting my teeth. "Hold my calls, Starla, I need to go over a few things with Cara before I take off."

"Anything for you, Braxton," she says. I nearly freeze on the spot, for the first time in my life I want to lay claim to a man. I envision myself plucking her eyes from her sockets so she can't look at my man like that ever again! And her sultry tongue, yeah—that has to go too. Braxton tugs on my arm causing my feet to move from their firmly planted spot.

He leads me into his office and I catch Paisley's grin as she goes into Twisted's. Before the respective doors close, she winks. He walks over to his chair and says, "C'mere, sweetheart."

I am so out of my element here! Graham was strictly a missionary man, and from my experience the other night, not a very good one. I slowly walk over to his chair and he gently pulls me onto his lap.

194

"Kiss me, Cara," he commands. All thoughts of Starla disappear with his demand.

Damn! His voice alone makes my engines rev, but couple it with the ride back and I'm about to combust. I lean down to kiss him and find his hands have moved to my hair, removing my braid. "Love your hair, sweetheart," he murmurs against my lips. He deepens the kiss and I find myself lost, surrounded by him. I can feel my heart skip a beat in anticipation of what is yet to come.

Before I know what has happened, I'm shirtless and he has unsnapped my bra. "Braxton! I... I didn't think you were serious." Deep down however, I knew he was, why am I in denial when it comes to this man and his wayward ways?

"Sweetheart, I'm always gonna be serious when it comes to my dick in your pussy." With no warning, he nuzzles my neck causing me to arch my head back. I had no damn idea that spot was an erogenous zone, but somehow, he knows. My bra is now somewhere on the floor, having joined my shirt and both of his hands are stroking my breasts, causing my nipples to pebble and harden beneath his touch. "Feels so good," I moan.

"Stand up, sweetheart," he murmurs before taking one of my nipples in his mouth. Yeah right, stand up now? My legs are fucking shaky and I'm pretty sure that Niagara Falls has taken up roost between my legs.

Shakily, I stand and watch as he quickly unsnaps and unzips my jeans before pulling them, along with my underwear, down my legs and off onto the floor. I'm now standing here naked in his office and he's looking at me like he grabbed the brass ring. With no warning, he lifts me onto his desk, his shoulders between my legs to spread them apart. Seconds later, his tongue and lips are on me, moving from back to front as though he has all the time in the world. "Damn, sweetheart, you're soaked. Thinking you like riding more than you let on."

He continues his ministrations and I find my hands moving to my breasts. They ache and I'm hoping I can soothe them somehow, even as I start writhing on his desk. I've never felt so out of control as I do right now. When first one finger and then a second enter me, I feel my back arching off the desk. "Fuck...Braxton...what are you doing to me?" I moan out. "I can feel myself clenching around your fingers, I need more, Braxton, I need you inside of me."

Braxton

My sweet girl *can* talk dirty and I find myself harder than a steel pipe. I can feel her pussy fluttering so I increase my pace, curling my fingers until I find that spot I know will drive her up the wall. Thanking God and Twisted for the foresight to put in soundproofing, I concentrate on her clit, wanting one orgasm at least to ease my way into her. "Let go, sweetheart, I want to hear you."

Her moans become screams and I feel her pussy as it pulsates around my fingers. When she screams out my name all bets are off, "Good girl," I whisper as I quickly unzip my jeans and pull out my rock hard dick. "Now, ride me, fuck yourself with my dick, Cara."

The look on her face is priceless and I can tell she has no clue what I mean. Good thing I signed up for a lifetime of showing her. I grab her hands in mine and pull her so she's once again straddling my lap. Lifting her slightly, I place my dick at her entrance and surge upward while grabbing her hips and pulling her down at the same time. Once I'm fully seated inside, and silently counting back from a hundred to keep from losing it, I take her hands and put them on either side of me then put mine back on her waist and begin raising her up and down.

"Oh, I like this," she moans, a sparkle in her eyes. I lean back just a little to change the angle and her dick-perfect lips form an "O" before she moves her hands to my shoulders and starts moving, circling her hips every time she comes down.

Seconds.

Minutes.

Hours.

I don't know, and don't particularly care, as I watch this woman come into her own, riding my dick like she's been doing it all her life. She's taking charge and owning me as if I'm her bronco bull, and I'm silently begging for the clock to never run out. I can feel the flutters in her pussy so I lean down and take one of her nipples in my mouth and suck hard. "Braxton!" she yells out, her orgasm crashing over her. I manage to keep my man card— barely—by lasting three more thrusts before I'm calling out her name.

Totally spent, she collapses on me and I pull her slight frame into my arms. Tilting her chin, I take her lips and kiss her, mimicking everything we just did while we both ride out the aftershocks of our respective orgasms. "That was...that was...hell, I don't have the words," she murmurs once we break apart.

Scooping her up along with her clothes, I walk to the bathroom I have in my office and sit her on the counter. Our *activities* have left us both sweaty and sticky, so I grab a washcloth and get it wet before gently cleaning first her and then myself. "If we had time, we'd grab a quick shower," I tell her as I help her stand so she can get dressed.

"A... a shower?"

"Yeah, sweetheart, a shower." I grin, watching my woman's face and upper chest go a pretty shade of pink. She has no idea the thoughts that have run through my mind where she's concerned. As she dresses—I can't help but think, as I watch her ass swaying in the air, that I'd like my brand to be right there—so I can admire it every time I take her from behind. Knowing I'm running out of time, I quickly dress but I mentally start designing her ink.

Looking over at the clock as I pull my last boot on, I realize I'm going to have to head out and I sigh. "Hate to say this, Cara, but I'm going to have to head out."

She looks at me in the mirror where she's trying to tame her curls back into a braid. "Leave it down."

"But everyone will know what we've been doing!" she exclaims.

"Sweetheart, I don't give a fuck what anyone thinks and neither should you. And if anyone says anything, you let Twisted know." Patting her on the ass, I say, "C'mon, walk me out to the warehouse, I want to show you my home away from home for the next week."

I smile at the look on her face when she sees the cab. Twisted and I had made the decision to invest in our long-haul trucks and each one is customized to include a mini eating area that converts to a comfortable double bed, a small refrigerator and a working stove and sink. We even have a stand-up shower and commode. Yeah, it was a hefty investment, but both of us had the money and wanted our drivers to be comfortable. "Wow, it's

199

like a small hotel room on wheels!" she exclaims, looking around. I imagine us on the road, her cooking while I'm driving, then later us wrapped in each other's arms as we snuggle into the small bed. Shaking myself out of my thoughts, I turn and respond to her last statement.

"It is, yes. This one is assigned solely to me, so I keep things in here all the time in case I'm called out to handle a run unexpectedly. Then I don't have to pack and shit."

"How many like this do you have?"

"Hatch has one and so does Chief, since they're the other two who handle the long distance runs. Well, actually, Hatch mostly does our local runs, but we've picked up more than Chief and I can handle, so we have him back in rotation with us. Once we hire more drivers to take some of these runs, we're going to see whether or not they want one for themselves and if they do, we'll get them the deal we got. We will most likely cough up the money up front, but we'll make up a contract to where they pay it out to us in installments. I think if someone has ownership, they're more liable to take care of it."

"I agree, Braxton. So, am I allowed to kiss you bye?"

"Wouldn't let you walk back inside otherwise, sweetheart. Now, c'mere."

Long delicious minutes are spent as I try to convey everything I'm feeling in this kiss. I know it's too soon for the usually forbidden "L" word, but the way I'm feeling? It won't be long. "I'll try and call when I've stopped for the night after I've talked to Mom and Lily."

"Okay."

"What time does Luca go to bed?"

"I try to get him down around seven thirty or eight o'clock so he gets a good night's sleep. Although, that wasn't what happened last night, and we paid for it this morning. It was more around nineish when I finally got Luca down, and a little later than that for Ray."

"No wonder they were all cranky this morning!"

"Yeah, it was definitely a morning to remember," she says with a wry grin.

Twisted, coming up alongside the cab, says, "You ready, man? Got the papers up on the dash and the customer's expecting you in two days. Drive safe."

"Will do. Keep things running here, yeah?" I reply.

"Always. Don't worry about your girl here, either. Me and Paisley will make sure she knows the ropes."

I hop up into the cab and see she's moved to stand next to Twisted. With a wave of my hand, I start it up and head out. For the first time since starting this company, I'm wishing I wasn't one of our drivers.

CHAPTER TEN

Caraleigh

Two weeks later

Braxton's one week trip has extended to two weeks, thanks to a screw-up on the customer's end. Several parts they thought they had in stock had been sold and they had to wait for more to arrive. He's been calling every night and we've spent hours getting to know one another better. But damn, I miss the man himself. Is it love? I have no clue even though DJ says yes. All I know is he's the first thing I think of in the morning and the last thing I think about when I lay down to go to sleep.

We've settled into a routine of sorts. DJ is feverishly working to finish her latest book so that she can go home, pack and be back before the edits come back. Nan takes the kids to school every day and picks them up and each night the six of us eat dinner together. The kids have fallen in love with her and I'm glad that they have that since my mom isn't as close as I'd like. She kept Luca when I moved in but stayed at a hotel, and now? She's on a cruise or something. Shaking my head to clear my thoughts, I recheck the figures for payroll and hit the button. I'm still a little shocked at what my salary is and tried to tell both Braxton and Twisted it was too much, but they both say it's comparable to industry standards. Whatever that means.

Once all the checks have printed, I take them into Twisted's office so he can sign them. "Twisted? How does this work with Braxton being out of town? Don't the checks need two signatures?"

"Law'll be here shortly to sign them, Cara. All of the officers in the MC are on the account as approved signature bearers, so we can handle anything. Speaking of, I need to get you on the list as well so you can handle the smaller shit. Those checks only need one signature once the invoice has been approved."

"Um, okay, that's fine."

"Gotta get your bonding approval first, then we'll get it taken care of, okay?"

I nod because what else can I do? My employment paperwork was like navigating through a Masters thesis and I had to go and get fingerprinted and have a background check run so they could add me to the bond they hold.

"We'll get these signed and hand them out. Anything you can think of I need to know or pass along?"

I had been thinking of a few things and ran them by Braxton who agreed, so I nod. "Yeah, I talked to Braxton and he liked the idea, so he said to tell you.

What if we find a company that can produce t-shirts, polo-style shirts and even tank tops with the company logo? Maybe even jackets? Not calling it a company uniform by any means, but since we've got such a relaxed dress code, we could have them in a variety of colors."

"Would we buy the employees' shirts or would they?"

"Kind of both, actually. Each employee would get an initial 'shopping allowance' and then yearly, a stipend to either replace anything that has worn out or to purchase more. If they want other non-clothing items, they would cover that cost. Or, y'all could come up with some incentive programs and give them away. Or give them away to customers. I don't know, just thought it would be something different."

"I like it. Go ahead and do your research, Cara, and get me the information. We'll take it to church and vote on all of it and let you know what the final decision is, okay?"

"Works for me. Paisley and I are heading out for lunch, would you like to go?"

"Naw, Law and I have to take care of this and then we'll grab something. You two go and have a good time. And Cara? You know you don't have to watch the clock with us, right?"

"I'm trying to set a good example, Twisted."

"It's appreciated, but in many ways, we're on biker time around here. Our customers know that and so do the employees. If you've got something to do, you do it, just make sure I know you'll be in late. Or, if you're done with everything, take off for the day."

"Got it. Thanks." There is always loads of work to get done on my end, so I doubt I'll ever be leaving early. Paperwork, phone calls, research, marketing, payroll, keeping up with the employees' daily time cards...always something to do, and never enough working hours in the day.

"No problem, Cara. We're happy as hell you're here. Making my life a helluva lot easier, that's for sure."

I smile as I head out the door and back to my office to grab my purse. I'm pretty much done for the day—for once, so I lock up my office and stick my head back in to say, "If you're serious about what you've just said, I'll drop Paisley back when we're done with lunch and take off for the weekend."

"What about your check? This is the live one before your direct deposit starts."

"You can give it to Hatch to bring over, he and DJ are going out tonight."

"That works. Have a great weekend Cara."

205

Lunch was a lot of fun. DJ was able to break away, citing the fact that she 'had to eat' and we've spent the past hour eating chips and salsa and laughing our asses off. One of the funniest things, though, is that apparently Twisted is a soccer coach for the eight and under youth. Both DJ and I decided that when sign-ups start, we're going to get the kids involved. It'll be good exercise for them and they'll learn how to have good sportsmanlike conduct. Paisley has promised to let him know so he asks specifically for the kids. We keep this up and the Rebel Guardians will have their own team!

Now, after a quick trip to the grocery store, I'm headed home. With DJ going out, and likely staying at the clubhouse tonight, and Nan heading out of town for a 'girls weekend away' which I feel she wholly deserves, I'll be holding the fort down with all three kids. I still don't know when Braxton is due in. Could be late tonight, could be tomorrow. So, I needed provisions. Juice boxes and chips for the kids, ice cream and soda for me.

Pulling into my parking space, I grab the bags and head inside. I see DJ in the kitchen trying to referee the three kids and say, "Hey, what's going on in here?"

She gives me a grateful look and replies, "They want to do some experiment that they did in school today, but don't believe me when I tell them we don't have all the stuff."

"Y'all go on now and either play out in the backyard or go watch a movie. Otherwise, you'll all be in bed before DJ leaves." Three sets of eyes look at me before they turn without a word and head into the backyard.

"Thanks, girl. I gotta finish getting ready. Hatch'll be here any time now."

"Y'all seem to be getting along pretty well," I say to her.

"We are, actually. He seems to like my sassy mouth," she replies with a grin.

"Mmhmm, and your rocking body too, I'm sure," I reply, wiggling my eyebrows up and down.

"Says the pot to the kettle. I know you haven't shared and that's okay because some things should stay between a couple, but damn, girl, I think you're getting it good."

I know my blush is a dead giveaway as DJ breaks out into laughter. "Not going there with you."

Her tinkling laugh follows her as she heads back upstairs to get ready.

Once I finally got the kids settled, I took a long hot bubble bath and am now sitting in my bed reading while a mindless show is playing on the television. Hearing my phone chime, I put my e-reader aside and grab it and see a text from Braxton.

Braxton: You up?
Cara: Yes, just reading
Braxton: Come to your door

I fly down the stairs to the front door, then look out the peephole to see him standing there. Uncaring that I'm in my pajamas, I quickly unlock the door to let him in. As soon as he closes the door and locks it, I'm in his arms with his lips claiming mine. "Missed you," he murmurs, covering my face with kisses as his hands hold me close.

"Missed you, too," I reply, my own hands running up and down his back. "You look tired."

"I'm beat but when I went to my house, I realized that Mom was gone and you had all the kids. Figured that DJ was probably with Hatch, at least for the night, and decided there was nowhere else I wanted to be than here with you."

"C'mon, handsome, let's get you upstairs then, shall we?" I take him to my room and start to strip him of his clothes.

"A man could get used to this," he says as he runs his fingers through my hair. I'm down on my knees, face to crotch as I'm divesting him of his boots so that he can take his jeans off.

"Wasn't exactly what I had in mind, Braxton, but I could be convinced to accommodate your needs. I had thought you might enjoy a long warm shower to scrub the road off you...and maybe, um—maybe I could join you...you know, scrub your back and all that."

"Baby, you can join me anytime, anywhere, and anyplace that I am. And you're right, a shower sounds wonderful. I'm exhausted though, so I'd love for you to join me in the shower...two birds-one stone and all that," he says as he helps me remove the last of his clothing. Raising up to my feet, I raise up on my toes and plant a kiss under his jaw.

"Poor baby, let's get you clean, satisfied and in bed for the night...shall we?" I say as I turn around and hold my hand out for him. He takes my hand and I lead him into the bathroom. I start the shower as he stands there watching me, as I slowly and seductively as I can remove my clothing. I'm enjoying this new freedom I've found when it comes to my sexuality. I've come to learn during my time with Braxton, that I definitely love sex with my man and the way he makes me feel. Feeling brazen and bold, I climb into the shower and look over my shoulder, "Are you coming in to join me?"

"Fuck yeah, I am," he says as he climbs in the shower with me. I turn on my multiple shower heads so that we both get nice and wet. I grab my body wash and lather it onto my loofa, I start to run it across his shoulders and down his chest—but skip the most important area. I'm saving that for later. Then I get down on my knees and wash his legs and feet. "Turn around, Braxton," and he does as I ask with no questions or demands of his own. I stay down and work my way up his body, once I reach his shoulders I hang the loofa on my wrist and begin to massage his shoulders, they're very tense and I'd like for him to go to bed as relaxed as possible.

"That feels so good, Cara." Mentally high-fiving myself, I continue until I feel the knots loosen under my fingers. Still skipping the part I want to touch the most, I grab my bottle of shampoo, get a healthy amount on my hands. and I lather it up and run my fingers through his hair, loving the thickness of it as I massage his scalp. He has a head full of hair and has even begun growing a beard, which I'm finding I love. I have never been a beard lover on men, but on him—wow.

Once I have him rinsed off, I get down on my knees once again and turn his body. I'm not very experienced at what I want to do next to him, but I want to taste him, to feel him get excited in my mouth. I've never desired this type of thing before, but with him—I want to gift him everything I have within me to give. He's already hard and long, and my mouth waters in anticipation.

"Hmm...Cara, what are you thinking about so hard down there, beautiful?" he asks me and instead of answering him I wrap my hand around him and pull him into my mouth.

"Holy fucking shit, Cara!" he calls out as I swipe my tongue down his impressive length. His shout encourages me to keep going and exploring what makes him excited the most. I pump my hand up and down lower at his shaft as my tongue and mouth work him over. He's too big for me to fit completely in my mouth, but what I can fit has become an addiction to me. I take his head and suck just it and he throws his head back in one of the loudest moans I've heard from him to this date. I feel energized by this and using my tongue I trace the contours of his head. He's nice and warm and I'm enjoying getting to know this side of my inner sex diva.

"Cara, don't stop. Fuck me!" He only allows me to bob my head a few more times before he grabs me underneath my arms and pulls me up as if I weigh nothing. Wrapping my arms and legs around him, I'm shocked when he pushes my back against the cold tile in the shower.

"Fuck, that's cold!" I tell him, but lose all feeling once he slams himself inside of me. Now it's my turn to scream out in pleasure. He's frantic in his ministrations, he's pumping in me hard and fast and I know he's chasing his release. Wanting to join him when he comes, I put my finger on my clit and do what he does to me that always causes me to detonate. I apply pressure and use circular motions while using two of my fingers.

"Yes, baby, get yourself there. God damn that's fucking hot! I could sit and watch you play with that pretty pussy of yours all day long," he moans out. Then out of nowhere it hits me like a tsunami and I scream out his name...and maybe a few other words along the way, but who can think of what is being said when you're in a state of bliss this deep?

"If this is the way you welcome me home, I need to go out of town more often."

Not finding his statement amusing at all I slap his shoulder and tell him, "Not on your life, buster!" He pulls out of me and we both let out a groan of disappointment at our loss. We clean ourselves up, get out and dry off. Grabbing my nightclothes from the bathroom vanity I redress for bed and watch as Braxton pulls his boxer briefs back on. I wrinkle my nose at the thought that he's putting back on dirty shorts.

Noticing my displeasure he smiles at me and says, "Don't worry, they're clean." He turns off the bathroom lights and leads me to bed.

Once we climb in the bed, he pulls my back to his front and nuzzles my neck. "This right here, this is what makes coming home worth it." Not knowing what to say, I snuggle deeper into his body. Not long after, I feel his breathing even out and hear his soft snores. At this moment I realize, that he is what is worth risking my heart for. This is my home, where I want to be.

Caraleigh

Six weeks later

I'm staring at my computer wondering how in the hell I can even see, my head is pounding so bad. The past three weeks have been rough as some virus and then strep went through the school. All three kids came down with it, one after the other and then poor Lily got strep for the second time. Nan set up a sick bay, keeping the kids there and tending to them during the day so DJ and I could work. They're all finally back at school and Nan has been busy disinfecting all three households to 'break the cycle' or so she says. I think she just likes to help.

Braxton's out of town again, and I'm missing him something fierce. Hopefully, he'll be home tonight. He mentioned having a surprise for me which has my curiosity roused. When my phone rings and I see it's Nan, I grab it, worried that one of the kids has relapsed.

"Nan? Are the kids okay? Please tell me we're not going into round three of this crap."

"Cara?" Her voice sounds funny, almost as if she's crying.

"Nan? What's wrong?" Not sure of what's going on but positive I'll need to leave, I put my phone on speaker and start shutting stuff down. "Talk to me, please."

"It's...it's Luca. Honey, you need to get to the hospital."

Luca? My breath leaves me in a whoosh and I slump back into my chair. "Nan?" I know my voice is shaky but we're talking about my boy here. My feelings of being sick are pushed to the wayside as I realize that she said I had to get to the hospital. "I'm on my way."

"Twisted!" I yell out. I know I won't be able to drive, not in this condition.

"Darlin', what's wrong?" he says as he comes running into my office.

"Nan just called and said I needed to get to the hospital, something to do with Luca."

"C'mon, Cara," he says, grabbing my jacket.

The drive to the hospital seems to take forever, even though I know it's mere minutes away. Twisted has barely stopped the truck by the emergency room doors when I'm jumping out and rushing into the ER. "I'm...I'm here for Luca Jensen," I tell the clerk.

"Right this way, ma'am," a nurse says. "Please, follow me."

"What...what happened?"

Twisted, coming in behind me, pulls me close as the nurse tells us what happened. "A group of kids were coming back across to the school in the crosswalk when a car hit them." Thank God his arm was around me because I nearly fall to my knees.

"Your son pushed two little girls out of the way, otherwise, they would be here as well," the nurse continues. *Lily and Ray! Oh my God, I need to call Braxton and DJ!*

I must've said that out loud because Twisted tells me, "I've got it, Cara, you go see your boy," as I go to leave I notice Paisley comes rushing in and pulls me to her arms.

"C'mon, girl, I'm here," she says. Pulling out of Twisted's embrace she takes my hand as we follow the nurse back to the bays. We finally reach one and she pulls back the curtain and I see Nan sitting next to the bed where my sweet boy lays. Nan has tears running down her face, most likely feeling guilt for Luca being harmed.

"Oh, Luca," I breathe out. He's got cuts and abrasions and his right leg is in some sort of splint.

Nan looks at me and stands, pulling me into her arms. "They've got him medicated but he's going to need surgery, the doctor was waiting for you to get here to give your permission."

"Is he...is he going to be okay?"

"He's going to be fine, Cara. Let me get the nurse so we can get him squared away."

The next few minutes seem to go in a rush as the nurse comes in to get my signature then he is whisked away to surgery, leaving me feeling bereft. I need Braxton, I need him to hold me and assure me that my little boy is going to be okay.

215

Braxton

After receiving the phone call, I erratically drive to get to my girls and Luca as quickly as possible. Arriving at the hospital, I make my way to the room that Twisted said they were now in, my heart in my throat. *He put himself in the path of the car to protect the girls.* I take a deep breath when I get to the room, I have to be strong for that little boy and also his mom. Quietly opening the door, I see Cara curled around him in the bed and his leg elevated with a neon blue cast from his toes to his thigh. The sight before me nearly has me crumbling to my knees in thanks that he's alive, and other than a few broken bones he's going to be just fine.

"Hey, sweetheart," I whisper as I kiss her temple.

"Braxton?" Her voice is all sleepy and despite the situation, I can feel my body reacting.

"I'm here, I got here as quickly as I could."

Pulling a chair next to the bed, I gently coax her onto my lap. I need to hold her and give her some of my strength. She's quietly crying now and I tug her closer, whispering nonsensical things in an attempt to soothe her. I feel her trembling in my arms and it's taking every ounce of strength and control not to go and hunt down this motherfucker. This person hurt my boy! Not to mention nearly took out my girl and Ralynn. If it wasn't for Luca's quick action there's no telling what would've happened. My thoughts drift to my mom, we're lucky this incident didn't give her a heart attack. I could've lost my entire family in one ill mentioned swoop! I'm so livid that I'm having a hard time not letting Cara feel my anxiety and anger.

"Mr. Braxton?"

Turning my head, I see Luca looking at me. He's glassy-eyed from the pain medicine but whatever he wants to say must be important. "Yeah, buddy?"

"I pushed Lily and Ray out of the way so they didn't gets hurt. Are...are they okay?"

Gulping at the vision he just gave me with a few simple words, I reply, "You did good, little man. The girls are okay, just some scrapes where they fell on the ground."

"Is my job to protects them," he murmurs, his eyes closing as he succumbs to sleep.

When I got Twisted's call, my heart dropped imagining the worst. As I drove back, grateful I was closer to home than any of them realized, I got constant updates from him, Mom, and finally Cara. I think my woman held on as long as she could if her tears are any indication. So fucking strong, my Cara. This solidifies any thoughts that have been running through my head the last several weeks. It's time to make them officially mine, in the eyes of the club, and the law. Nothing will hold me back or stop me, Cara and Luca will bear my last name and no one will ever question what they mean to me. Just as those thoughts enter my head, Cara stands up with her hand plastered over her mouth as she makes a mad rush for the attached bathroom.

I pull a washcloth from the cabinet and walk into the bathroom, my only thought is to help her. I pull her hair back and put the cool washcloth on the back of her neck.

"I think the kids got me sick," she says standing up and flushing the toilet. I didn't notice before, but she looks really pale. Now I'm worried for her and Luca, knowing she won't go home to rest while Luca is still in the hospital, I leave her side with hesitation, but she seems to need some medical intervention, what better place to get that than in the place we are? I walk out into the hallway and stop the first nurse I come across.

"My fiancee, in this room here," I point out Luca's room. "Is very sick, do you have a doctor who could come check her out for me?"

"I'll see what I can do, it's against regulations to treat a patient who isn't registered, but seeing as y'alls son is just getting out of surgery, he may make an exception." I don't correct her on Luca being my son, because in my heart he already is and I thank her and go back to the room.

Once I make it over the threshold of the room I yell out in anguish when I notice Cara passed out cold on the floor. "Help! Somebody help me!"

CHAPTER ELEVEN

Braxton

There's a flurry of activity once several nurses and a doctor rush into the room, pushing me out of the way. I feel arms pulling me back and nearly swing out trying to get loose. Then I hear Twisted say to me, "Let them do their job, man, you could do her more harm than good at this point in time." Knowing he's right I back off and let them tend to my girl.

I look over to check on Luca and see his eyes open wide in alarm at seeing his mother laying on the floor unconscious. I immediately go over to his side and hold his hand, and I reassure him that his mother is going to be fine...I hope and pray that that's the truth. We both watch as Cara is put onto a stretcher and wheeled out of the room. I look up and notice Mom and Paisley both standing there looking lost...*welcome to the club*, I think.

"I knew she wasn't feeling well, Son, but I never imagined it was serious," Mom says ringing her hands together.

"This isn't your fault, Mom. Could you please stay with Luca so I can go check on her?"

"Of course, I will," she says as she comes to stand vigil at Luca's bedside. I lean down and brush a kiss over his forehead and tell him I'll be back as quickly as I can.

Rushing out the door a nurse comes up to me, "Do you know her medical history or if she's allergic to any meds?"

I'm getting ready to tell her that I don't when I hear a voice behind me say, "I do." I turn to look for who said that and see DJ striding my way with purpose in every step. Hatch is trailing behind her with a look of concern on his face.

When DJ finishes answering the nurse's questions, she turns and looks at me, "Tell me what happened." I tell her about Cara getting sick, looking pale and finish with finding her on the floor. She has a twinkle in her eye and I nearly tell her off until I hear the words that come out next. "You know, this is exactly what it was like when she first got pregnant with Luca."

My eyes widen as it sinks in what she said. "Pregnant...Luca," I mumble out.

"Yes, sir, this is exactly what happened. We rushed her to the ER then too," she says with excitement in her voice.

"Are you...are you trying to tell me she's pregnant? With my baby?"

"No, I'm telling you this is what happened with Luca, same symptoms and her body did the same exact thing. And it's the milkman's, of course it would be yours if she is, you moron." I don't even care that she's calling me names, all I'm visualizing is Cara round with my child growing inside of her. I envision a little girl who looks just like her with pigtails and a goofy grin, sitting on her hip as we play with the other kids.

"Wow," is all I can manage. "And I know if she's pregnant it's mine! Give me a break, woman, I just found out I might be a dad again!" I hear Hatchet's laughter as I leave the two of them, once again on a mission to find my woman.

When I finally find her room, with no help from the staff I might add, I see a nurse taking vials of blood, checking her blood pressure and examining her eyes while the doctor looks over her chart. "Has she not woken up yet?"

"Not yet, sir, do you have any idea what symptoms she's been displaying?" the doctor asks.

"I've been on the road for work, but when I talked to her she's complained of an upset stomach. We've had strep and a virus running through the household." I'm looking at the nasty bruise coming up on the side of her face and cringe, knowing it's going to hurt.

"I don't believe this is strep or a virus or she wouldn't have lost consciousness. Is there any possibility that she could be pregnant?"

"There is," I tell the young doctor that's been grilling me with endless questions.

221

"I'd say so with the way you two go at it like a bunch of teenagers," I hear DJ say. I turn around and glare at her, normally this would cause people to cower in fear from me, but she just smiles at me.

"Get the lab to check for pregnancy, iron levels and for possible diabetes."

"Diabetes!" I yell out.

"Just as a precaution, sir," he says to me as he dismisses his nurse with his instructions. "She's stable, vitals are good...we'll know more once she wakes up and we get her results back. For now, let's let her sleep since her body seems to need it and we'll keep checking on her." He then leaves the room and me to my thoughts. Pregnant, could I really be so lucky as to have my child growing in her belly?

An hour later, Cara opens her beautiful eyes and looks around the room. She notices me sitting in the chair beside her with my hand in her own. As she takes stock of where she is she begins to panic and tries to get out of bed. "Take it easy, baby," I tell her.

"Luca..."

"Is fine, Mom and DJ are with him. He's sleeping soundly and is recovering nicely. They're going to keep him overnight for observation, but will be releasing him in the morning. He has a room being set up for him right now, I had them get him a private room. I don't see either of us wanting to leave his side any time soon. Now, let's talk about you."

"What happened? I don't remember anything after getting sick in the bathroom."

"You passed out, taking ten years off my life and adding some grey hair to my head," I say trying to lighten the mood. "Can you tell me what's been going on with you while I was away?"

"Well…" she starts to say as the door to the room opens abruptly.

"It's good to see you awake, Mrs. Jensen, you gave your fiancée here quite the scare," the doctor says to her as he opens her chart. "I have the results from your labs back here. It looks like you're pregnant, we'd like to schedule an ultrasound before we release you with a prescription for vitamins and folic acid." He carries on as if he didn't just drop the ultimate bomb in our laps.

"Did you—did you just say pregnant?" she asks the doctor, but her eyes are all for me.

"I did, congratulations. We'll be checking to see how far along you are and hopefully you're far enough along that we can hear the heartbeat today. That should settle some of the father-to-be's ruffles."

"Braxton." I stop her with my finger to her lips and smile over at her.

"You've made me the happiest man on the planet, sweetheart, the rest we can talk about later. Let me enjoy this moment with you before we deal with anything else."

"Okay," she responds with a small timid smile of her own. I look over and see a nurse wheeling in a machine, I somewhere in the back of my mind remember this from when Lily was expected. It has a small screen and a bunch of gadgets, but all I care about is that this contraption is going to let Cara and I see the life inside of her that we created together.

Cara is instructed to lift up her gown to expose her belly, so I tuck the blanket securely around her lower region, I don't want this young guy to see all that is mine. Once she's situated, he pours a good amount of goo on her stomach, saying, "We'll try this way first, hopefully you're far enough along that we won't have to use the wand."

Wand? What wand? And why is it that I don't think I'd like the idea of using that? Cara leans over and whispers in my ear what it is and it entails, then she points it out to me and I call out, "I don't fucking think so!"

"Relax, Braxton, it doesn't hurt and you have to be so far along to use the probe that goes over the stomach."

"If you're not, we'll wait until you are," I tell her in no uncertain terms.

224

"Honey, there will be a lot more invasive things done to me during this pregnancy, you're going to have to get used to it if it's what's good for the baby."

"Or the mom," the nurse says. "We don't want to take any chances with their health," she states to me as if she's speaking to a small child. I glare over at her and she acts as if she didn't see it. I've had men piss themselves from just that look alone, and these women act as if it isn't scary as fuck. Crazy ass women! No self-preservation whatsoever.

"Ah, look at that, you're measuring in at nine-weeks and three days. See, we can see the baby perfectly. You can relax, Dad, no internal wand needed." Nine-weeks, three days—that means the first time we had sex I knocked her up. All of a sudden, I feel as proud as a peacock, I want to puff out my chest and shout from the rooftop.

"He looks like a very proud and happy man," the child doctor whispers to my woman. I scowl at him, he shouldn't be whispering anything to my woman. "Caveman to the core I see," the doctor says with a smile on his face, one I want to immediately knock off.

"Braxton! Did you just growl?" Cara says with disbelief in her voice. What does she expect? This kid is flirting with her right in front of me.

"No!" I say, suddenly feeling like I need to protect my family makers if the scowl on her face is anything to go by.

"Yes, you did! Am I going to have to go to all of my doctor appointments without you?"

The fuck she will! "Hell no!" I all but shout.

"Then you need to calm down with all of the growling and scowling looks. I'm sorry, doctor, he must've hit his head." Did she seriously just apologize for me? I mean I might be acting a little dominant where it comes to her, but I can't seem to help myself.

"Do not apologize for me, give me some time to adjust. Things will calm down once I have my ring on your finger and my patch on your back and skin. Until then, until that day comes, you need to bear with me, y'hear?"

"Braxton," she whispers, "did you take something? I'm worried about you right now, you've never acted like this before. Is this what I have to look forward to?"

"It is until..."

"I heard you! Until your ring is on my finger and I'm branded with your patch. Aren't those things we need to discuss first?"

"No."

"That's it? Just no?" she asks with an exasperated sigh.

"Right, we'll just leave the two of you alone to discuss this...here are a couple of pictures of your baby. Congratulations again," the doctor says handing me some black and white fuzzy pictures. I look down trying to decipher what is what.

"Hand them over, let me show you what is what," Cara says. She shows me the head, arms, feet and suddenly I realize, I was so wrapped up in myself that I missed hearing the heartbeat. I'm such a fucking fool!

I went home to check in on Lily and Mom. Mom has both of the kids so that DJ can stay at the hospital with Cara and Luca. As I'm about to enter his room I hear DJ say, "No, he did not!" then she starts laughing hysterically.

"Yes he did, I thought that poor doctor was going to piss his pants, right there and then. I don't know what got into him," Cara tells her friend. I don't want to eavesdrop on them, but I really want to hear what Cara says next.

"You do so, he told you what was going on with him."

"What? The caveman in him needs the ring and patch to know what I mean to him?"

"No, he needs those things to secure the fact that you're in this as deep as he is."

"He never mentioned marriage before, DJ, what if he only wants to marry me now because of the baby? I can't be in a marriage because of those reasons." Is that what she thinks?

I don't stop to think, I march into the room and say to her, "What have I ever done or said to you that makes you think I'd settle like that? I love you, Cara, that's why I want to marry you, that's why I want to give you my name and my patch...there is no other reason other than that... I. Love. You."

"Aaannnddd...that's my cue to go," DJ says as she stands, gives us both a hug and tells us congratulations as she scurries out of the room.

"You, you love me, Braxton?"

"I do, to the depths of my soul, you're my world. You, Lily and Luca...you three are my everything. I wake each morning, I breath and I exist, solely for y'all."

"I love you too, Braxton," she says as she leaps out of her chair and into my arms. "I love you so much!"

"I love you too, Daddy." And that's when it happens, that's when for the first time in my life I hit my knees, gravity taking me down by my son's bedside, and tell him how much I love him too.

"Marry me," I know this isn't the most romantic setting, but I feel the need to do this here and now. "Marry me, baby, make me the luckiest man in the world. Say yes, Cara, please say yes."

"Yes," she whispers with tears falling down her face, "I'd be honored to marry you, Braxton."

DJ

I couldn't help myself, I stand out in the hallway and listen to my best friend's dreams come true. No one deserves this more than them, I feel my phone vibrate in my pocket. I pull it out and read the text and I know that I need to go after, and get my happily ever after.

Hatchet: Coming home soon? I grabbed Ray from Nan and she's tucked in bed. I miss you baby

I leave the hospital with a smile on my face and a skip in my step. Nothing can be better than this, this new family that Cara and I have found ourselves in, they opened their arms and welcomed us in with no questions asked. My friend has found her forever love, now I need to go home and claim mine....

Me: On my way, missed you too, lover

CHAPTER TWELVE

Caraleigh

"His vitals all look good and we have his pain under control, I think we can let this young man go home," the doctor tells us after finishing with Luca's exam.

"Are you sure it isn't too soon?" I ask him, worried that it's too fast for Luca to be going home.

"I promise, Mrs. Jensen, I wouldn't be sending him home if he wasn't ready and I wasn't confident that he would be okay."

I turn my head when I hear screeching at the doorway. "What have you let happen to my grandson?" Seeing Graham's parents standing in the doorway of his room is the last thing I expected. "I told my son that you'd make a horrible mother! Look at him, if Graham hadn't died none of this would've happened to his boy. You don't deserve him, Caraleigh, you never deserved either of them."

"Now wait a goddamn minute!" Braxton stands from his chair, "Who are these people, Cara?" he practically shouts out. I can feel the anger rolling off of him.

"These would be Graham's parents," I whisper, afraid if I say it any louder I would have to admit to myself that my worst nightmares are actually here.

"And, who might I ask, is this man questioning who we are?" she asks snootily, causing Braxton to growl.

"I'm her fiancee, you don't get to come in here and question her or her ability at being a Mom!"

I go over and try to soothe the beast before he unleashes his fury on my in-laws. "Baby, it's okay...really, I'm used to them."

"Nobody treats you like that, Cara, no one!"

"Mmm...Momma?" Luca calls my name, but it comes out more like a question. "Why are they here?" That's a good question, one I'd like answered myself.

"Good question, Luca, what are you two doing here and how did you find out he was in the hospital?"

"Well, it isn't because *you* had the decency to call us and inform us our grandson was hit by a car!" he bitch has the nerve to scream.

"I'm going to have to ask that you stop screaming, or I'll have security escort you from the building," the doctor tells them.

"You will do no such thing," Mr. Jensen states, like he has all the authority here.

"I can and I will," the doctor spouts right back. "Nurse, get security up here."

"Now hold on a minute there," Mrs. Jensen says grabbing the nurse's arm as she tries to leave the room to do the doctor's bidding. "We have every right to be here and check on Luca."

"Remove your hand from my arm immediately," the nurse calls out. My mother-in-law does as instructed but gives me the ugliest look in return.

"This is all your fault," she says pointing a finger my way. "You ruined my son, I will not allow you to ruin my grandson as well." Oh yeah! Now I'm fighting mad.

"Doctor, would you kindly remove these people from my son's room?"

"Gladly," he tells me.

"About fucking time," Braxton says coming next to me and wrapping his arm around my waist, I notice his other hand is holding Luca's for support.

"Don't worry, Luca, Grandmother and Grandfather will make sure to be seeing you real soon. And we'll be removing you from your mother's care, looks like she can't take care of you responsibly or properly," Mrs. Jensen says as she grabs her husband and drags him out of the room.

"I don't want to go live with Grandmother and Grandfather!" Luca screams out at the top of his lungs. I rush to my boy to comfort him, but Braxton beats me to it with his next words.

"Not happening, buddy, I'll never let anything happen to you or your mother."

"Prowmise."

"I swear it to you, to both of you." I lean up and kiss Braxton underneath his chin.

"Thank you, baby," I say to him.

"If you two will be good for a minute, I'm gonna step out into the hallway and give Law a call."

"We'll be fine, baby."

Braxton

I pull my phone from my pocket still seething at the nerve of those assholes. I brush my finger over the screen to bring it to life, then I scroll down until I see Law's name. I press the call button and wait for him to answer.

"Axe, my man, what can I do for you today?"

"I need your help man, Caraleigh's dead husband's parents showed up here and were complete assholes, they made some threats, legal and otherwise."

"Lay it on me," he tells me and so I do. I tell him from the second they left the room until the moment the stupid cow dragged her husband from the room.

"Tell me, do they have a leg to stand on here?" I ask him desperately hoping for the answer I want.

233

"I don't see how they'd have any, let me look into them and see if they have any skeletons in their closet and I'll get back with you. And can you get Cara to get me a copy of his will? Don't worry, Braxton, I won't let these dipshits take Luca from you and Cara."

"Appreciate that man, anything you can do to end this before it begins would mean the world to Cara and myself. I'll get with her to get that copy for you as well. I don't want this touching her or Luca any more than it already has, if you get my drift."

"I get you, man, let me get off here so I can get to work on it. I will make this my top priority, that's a promise." We end the call, but I get in touch with both Twisted and Hatchet, and let them know of the morning's activities. I also want them watching for any outsiders coming around and asking questions. I will protect Cara and Luca with all that I am, and I will use any arsenal I have in my pocket to do so.

Four hours later, we finally make it home from the hospital. We have Luca's prescriptions in hand and he even has a wheelchair and crutches to accommodate him at school and home. I lay him on the couch so that he will be more comfortable than being held in my arms.

"Braxton, we can't be lugging him up and down those stairs, and he's not steady enough on his feet to do it all on his own. I guess we need to get him a bed made on the couch and bring down some of his stuff," Cara says to me, while chewing on her bottom lip. I notice she does this when lost in thought or if she's nervous about something.

"I have a better idea," I tell her. "What if we pull his bed down here along with some of his belongings and set him up in that corner over there," I say pointing to the one corner in the living room that isn't occupied by much. We can move her desk over and make plenty of room for him, so he still has his own little space.

"That would definitely make things easier for taking care of him, I could bed down at night on the couch, so I'll be close by."

"Or, we could get a monitor so you can hear him, you still need to get a good night's sleep to be any good to him, sweetheart." I don't like the idea of my woman sleeping on a couch.

"I'll need to contact the school so we can make sure they're prepared for him and the extra help he'll need. The doctor said he'll need to use the wheelchair at first, so someone will need to push him through the halls. Maybe I should just keep him home for a bit?"

"I think keeping him home for a couple of days is a good idea, plus it will give us time to go up to the school. Something needs to change, that accident should've never happened," I tell her.

"I agree, and I feel so guilty. I noticed his first week how unorganized and how short-staffed they were for watching the kids. I should've said something, made some demands, something."

"You can't put this on your shoulders, beautiful, as parents we trust the school to take care of our kids, it's their job to keep them safe while in their care. This is all on them, but there needs to be some demands made and compensation for their stupidity."

"I don't want any money from them, Braxton, I just don't want this to happen to someone else's child." My sweet, beautiful woman, always thinking of others.

"I didn't mean money sweetheart, but we're going to have Law pursue that for Luca's sake. We can put it up for his college fund or a bike fund."

"Um, just saying, Graham left me with enough that I never have to work again, and also set up a college fund up for Luca. And as far as that bike goes...that's a no-go."

"Well, he's going to get that other money, so maybe you let what he got from Graham grow and put this aside to take care of whatever else he might need. And, just saying, once I adopt him, he becomes the oldest son and my successor to the club so yeah, there's gonna be a bike in his future. Now, let's get you and Luca something to eat, you two must be starving."

"I's is, Daddy," Luca says. Every time he's called me daddy I feel my heart beat a little faster.

"Let me go grab Lily from Nan and I'll be right back and get my family fed."

"Yay! I wanna see my sister." This kid!

Caraleigh

When Braxton leaves to go get Lily, I pepper my son with kisses and go to give DJ a call. She and Hatchet are finally at her place to get her belongings to move here.

"Yo, bitch, what's this I hear about the in-laws from hell making an appearance at the hospital?"

"Well, hello to you too."

"Cut the crap and tell me what happened." And this is why she's my best friend. I lay it all out for her, their threats and accusations.

"You're fucking kidding me! I wanted to call as soon as I heard, but Hatch wouldn't let me. He told me...do you hear me, *told me,* I had to wait for you to call me when you were ready. What's up with that shit? You know me, no one tells me when I can and can't call my bestest. As soon as I told him that

237

he took my phone from me! Are you listening to me? Why are you laughing?"

I hold my stomach as I'm doubled over laughing, tears are running down my cheeks. That's some funny shit right there, just what I needed right now. "I can't believe he took your phone!"

"I know, right? What does he think he is, my daddy or something?"

I hear Hatchet in the background saying, "I got your daddy right here...do I need to prove something to you again gorgeous?" Uh-oh, shit, I better get off the phone before I overhear world war three happening.

"I know you did not just...eeekkk, put me down you neanderthal!" I hear as the line suddenly disconnects. I start laughing even harder, so hard in fact I'm having a hard time catching my breath and that's how Braxton finds me. At the kitchen table, doubled over trying to draw as much oxygen into my lungs as I possibly can.

"What happened? Cara, are you alright? Talk to me sweetheart." I hear the concern in his voice, and I try to tell him, but I can't get the words out.

"Is Momma gonnas be okay?" I hear Lily say and that brings my oxygen-deprived brain back on drive.

"I'm...o... okay, Lily, I promise. Your aunt DJ just made me laugh really hard," I say while drawing in a breath with each word that leaves my mouth.

Ralynn comes over to me, she had been staying with Nan, and wraps her arms around my shoulders and says as seriously as a six-year old can, "What's shes done now?"

"Nothing drastic, sweetie, your mom is just silly." With that she nods her head once, gives me a hug, then Lily does the same. Only Lily gives me a kiss on my cheek before they scurry away to sit with Luca. Once they're out of ear-shot, I tell Braxton about my phone call with DJ. By the end he's laughing as hard as I was.

"Mom made a lasagna and garlic bread and she has made a side salad to go with the meal, she is bringing it over in a few minutes. So, lucky y'all that you don't have to suffer through my cooking." I know he's joking with me, because he's a wonderful cook.

"I think we would've managed just fine," I tell him with a yawn.

"Why don't you go rest for awhile? Mom and I can handle the kids while you get a couple of hours of shuteye."

"I really need to be here for Luca," I tell him.

"Please, for me—for the baby." I put my hands over my stomach and his join me as he pulls me in close for a hug. I can't wait until we can feel the baby move.

"Alright, Braxton," I yawn again and realize he's right, I do need to lay down. He follows me upstairs, giving me the excuse that he needs to tuck me in and once we're in my room, he closes the door.

"We need to talk, sweetheart." Fuck, I hate *those* four words 'we need to talk'!

"About?" I ask even though I know I may dread asking the question.

"I spoke with Law and he's going to check into Graham's parents, and he also wants a copy of Graham's will so he can see exactly what's what."

"Oh, I have that in my lockbox stored in the closet!"

"Great, I'll grab it, get Twisted over here, and hand it off to him so he can deliver it to Law for us today. Did you call your parents and your brother?"

"DJ called them. Mom and Dad are out of the country until next week, but Chandler's on his way and should be here today. My parents will come as soon as they get back, which knowing Mom, means they could show up today as well."

I'm about to lay down when he pulls my shirt up. "What are you doing? I thought I was resting?"

"You are sweetheart, but you need to be comfortable," he says as he unclasps my bra. "Mmmm, like how these look," he murmurs as his fingers ghost over my overly-sensitive nipples.

"Whose version of comfortable are we talking about here, Braxton?" I tease him with a moan.

"Mine, of course, what else would there be, woman?" he states.

I'm lost in the sensation of his hands on me when I hear Lily yell, "Daddy! Someone's at the door!"

"Fuck," he mutters.

"Duty calls," I tell him.

"Yeah, yeah woman, get some rest. I'll come back up and get the Will and check on you soon," he says as he turns to walk out the door after giving me a kiss on my forehead. I watch him go out the door, then turn over, grab my huggy pillow to take his place, and fall into dreamland.

Braxton

This past week has been...hectic. Yeah, that's the word I'm going with because complete and utter chaos makes me sound like a pussy. Chandler arrived and then not twenty-four hours later, Cara's parents showed up on her doorstep. Between our two houses, everyone has someplace to sleep, but I'm realizing that I need to find a house for us—me, Cara, Lily and Luca. Mom has already told me that she plans to stay at the complex. When I pressed her, she said it was time. So, I put Mom and Paisley on the house hunt, telling them what I am looking for but stressing that they need to take Cara's wants into consideration as well. Today? We're going to

241

look at a farmhouse they found about ten miles away. It's got about ten acres, so plenty of room for the kids to play, which is a must, especially since we're going to be adding to the family in about seven months or so.

"You good, sweetheart?" I ask, glancing over at her.

"Hmm? Yeah, just thinking about how crazy it's been all week long. I'm grateful for the grands though, because I got some peace and quiet yesterday at the office so I could keep shit caught up."

"Honey, we made do before you started and would have muddled along until you got back."

"Um, no. I've worked my ass off to get the office organized so the invoices are paid timely and shit. Y'all had a hot mess going on!"

"We're so fucking glad you're there," I tell her.

"Yeah, yeah...you just like the perks of me being close to you on a daily basis." Shit, not just a daily basis, I like her near me on a minute by minute basis.

Well, she's got me there—I managed to coax her into my office yesterday for a 'business meeting'. Twice. Granted, it involved us being naked with her sprawled across my desk and then bent over my chair, but whatever. "I'll never complain about wanting you, sweetheart."

We pull up to the address I was given and I'm already impressed—a freshly-painted fence surrounds the property and older trees grace the driveway that I'm now pulling down. I hear her gasp when we finally see the house. It's a rambling farmhouse with what looks like a wraparound porch that's deep-set with a swing on one end and comfortable looking rocking chairs and a table on the other. I see a car there and realize that the real estate agent is waiting. Putting the truck in park, I get out then go and help Cara down. I'm a little surprised that she's showing already given that she's only a little over two months along, but she's got a small belly bump that has me worrying that she'll lose her balance and fall. So, I pull her close and walk up the porch.

The front door opens and we're greeted by a woman who is maybe five-foot tall and by the looks of it is probably as big around. "Hi, I'm Marie," she says, holding out her hand.

"I'm Caraleigh and this is Braxton, my fiancée," Cara replies, holding out her hand. "Thanks for meeting us here today."

"Your friends were rather insistent," Marie states.

"I'll just bet they were," I mutter knowing exactly how Mom and Paisley are when they set their minds to something. You get the two of them together, and watch out or they'd run you over before they even realized you were standing in their path of destruction.

243

"I'm going to sit out here and let y'all look at the house by yourselves. Let you get the feel for it, I find that people can tell if it's for them or not if they are alone with their significant other. If you have any questions, just let me know and I'll do my best to get them answered."

I nod to let her know we understand then lead my woman into the foyer. A living room and formal looking dining room are at the front of the open floor plan. There's a hallway that leads off to both the left and the right and when we explore, we find a full bath and three bedrooms. Damn, how big is this place again? The kitchen looks newly renovated, not that the rest of the house isn't top-notch, with hardwood floors throughout. French doors are off to one side and we walk out onto a deck that is screened in, with an outdoor grilling area on the other side of the screening. The backyard is fenced in and my mind immediately starts thinking of a dog for the kids, something I need to clear with Cara first in case she or Luca are allergic.

"Let's go check out the upstairs, sweetheart."

"I'm liking what I've seen so far, Braxton."

"Me too."

Back inside, we go to the staircase that's next to the entrance of the family room that has a beautiful stone fireplace. Already my mind has a fire going and my delectable minx laying in front of it, on a bare skinned rug, naked and waiting. Feeling my dick harden, I grab her hand and lead her up the stairs. "You okay, Braxton?"

"Gotta find some privacy, sweetheart." Her sideways glance at me as the blush starts up her face has me laughing.

"Are you serious?" she hisses out. "That woman is out on the porch! She'll be able to hear us Braxton!"

"Trust me, this won't take long," I tell her, going to the door furthest down the hallway. Awesome, it's the master suite. Pulling her in and closing the door, I slide my hands up the dress she has on until I reach her panties. "And from the feel of things, you're onboard," I whisper before kissing her. Unzipping my jeans, I pull out my dick while slipping her panties off and down her legs. I slip my hands under her ass and lift her against the door so I can slip my steel hard cock inside of her. "You're gonna have to be quiet, minx," I whisper as I thrust myself deeply inside of her tight, wet heat. Being inside her is what I imagine heaven must be like and as cheesy as it would sound if I said it out loud, every time feels like the first.

"I'll try," she says before moaning. Her sexy noises and moans whenever we're together are another fucking turn-on for me, and I find myself picking up my pace, rolling my hips each time I thrust inside.

"Touch yourself, sweetheart," I command before I nip and nuzzle at that spot on her neck that

245

turns her into a wildcat. When I feel her fingers there at her entrance, managing to stroking her own clit while she slides her hand up my dick every time I pull out, I nearly lose it then and there.

"Oh *God*, Braxton, I'm so close," she whisper-shouts. "I need more...harder...faster."

Whatever my woman wants, my woman gets. I'll do whatever it takes to give her as much pleasure as I'm capable of, her satisfaction is my number one priority. I increase my pace and thrusts harder and faster, until my rhythm becomes sporadic and demanding. I feel her pussy begin to flutter, "C'mon, baby, give it to me beautiful," I say before capturing her lips with mine. My woman's a bit of a screamer and there's no way I want Marie to hear or know what we're doing, although I suspect she'll figure it out when we finally manage to get ourselves downstairs again.

My mouth captures her screams and four...five...six thrusts later, she captures my moans. Breathlessly, I let her legs down, keeping hold of her until she catches her balance. "Shit, baby, I didn't think about the fact you have no way to clean up."

"I've got it," she says, leaning down to pick up the purse she dropped, "just give me a second to get my land legs back."

Her comment catches me off guard—my woman doesn't realize how fucking funny she is at times—and I burst out laughing. I guess what they say is true, mothers are always prepared for anything and everything that could possibly happen.

"What? You know what you do to me!" she retorts before going over to the bathroom. "Oh thank goodness," she says before closing the door. I have no idea what she's found, but hopefully it'll help her clean up. Normally I do that for her because I can't help but want to take care of her.

When she comes out, her hair tamed and dress back in place, I grin. She still has that well-loved, thoroughly-fucked look I like seeing on her. "Thinking we just christened one room," I tell her, taking her hand and leading her out, "let's go see the other bedrooms, shall we?" She rolls her eyes at me and I can't help but smile at the action.

I'm fucking impressed with the girls. They found a house that will be absolutely perfect. In addition to the three bedrooms downstairs, there's a master suite upstairs, a 'sitting area' in the hall by the stairs where I can envision a television and comfortable chairs for the kids, five more bedrooms with two having a Jack and Jill bathroom set-up, and an attic door. The attic is finished with regular flooring and walls which could always be finished out into bedrooms if we have more kids. For the time being, we can make it into a playroom for Lily and Luca. Plus, there is plenty of room left for storing all that shit that families seem to accumulate.

247

We go back downstairs and I find another door in the kitchen. Opening it, I see it goes to a basement and we head down to see what there is down there. Holy shit—it's fully finished and I can picture a pool table and a mini-bar for those times when the guys want to come and watch the game. I'm excited at the possibility of having my very own man-cave, fully stocked and waiting for me to fill it with my brothers, beer, dartboard and a flat screen television set.

"Sweetheart? What do you think?"

"Braxton, I absolutely love it. I mean, it's got everything we wanted, including a mudroom off the laundry room." Yeah, that little hallway off the kitchen goes to the garage. There's even a bathroom there complete with a stand-up shower! Her voice breaks into my thoughts when she says, "Can we afford this?"

I think about what she said. It's somewhat pricey, but I've got money saved and I know she does as well. "Honestly? I think between what you and I both have tucked away, we can pay for it outright and we'll still have a nest egg."

"Do you know how many Christmas trees we're going to need?" *Christmas trees? What the fuck? Where...how...when did Christmas trees enter this conversation?*

"What are you talking about?"

"Well, we'll need one in that front room so it can be seen from the street, one in the family room where we'll probably put the presents, one upstairs in that sitting room for the kids to decorate, and one down in the basement in that awesome game room I can see you plotting," she replies. Fuck. My. Life. Four trees? Then again, we both have stuff we'll be bringing from both of our households, so I'm sure it won't be too bad. "If that's what you want, sweetheart. Let's go talk to Marie, okay? Then we have another appointment."

"What other appointment?"

"We need to go see about our marriage license."

CHAPTER THIRTEEN

Caraleigh

Marriage license? But I don't wanna be a fat pregnant woman when I marry him! "Uh, Braxton? I don't want to be all poofy when we get married. I thought we would wait until after the baby was born."

"Not happening, sweetheart. You'll have my rings and my last name before that sweet addition comes into this world."

I glare at him and he leans down and kisses me. "I figured we get the license and take the kids and go to the courthouse, unless you want something fancy. Then, we can have a cut ceremony at the clubhouse. I told you—I won't be happy until the woman I love is wearing my ring, my cut and my ink. We might have to wait on the ink until after the baby is born, but two outta three ain't bad."

Oh this alpha man of mine! He makes me smile even when I want to be mad. "I see."

"Glad we're on the same page now. Then, I figured since the kids are squared away, we can go to the clubhouse, maybe get in a nap in my room."

Nap. Ha! I know that man has sex on the brain. Again. Of course, with the pregnancy hormones kicking in, the minute he said nap, my nipples pebbled and I could feel myself getting wet again. I had no idea until he came along that I had such a sex drive! Then again, I'm finding out that even though I was married before, I had no clue how much *fun* could be had, either! "Yeah, I probably will need a... nap by then," I tell him, a grin playing on my lips.

"Yeah, my little minx, I'll be sure you're taken care of properly," he says with a smirk. "Now, let's get a move on."

Marie is stunned when Braxton makes the offer, in cash. Granted, he took off about twenty thousand and she says, "I need to call the sellers. Not sure they will come off the selling price, but since you want to pay cash and they're in a bit of a bind, it may be a go. Can I call you in a little while? I need to go back to the office to get their information and send them over the offer."

"That'll be fine. We have some other errands to run, but you have my number."

I look at him in amazement. Then I think of how much my life has changed, for the better, since moving here. My son is happy, I have a wonderful man, new daughter, a completed family waiting...just for me.

We've gone to the courthouse and gotten the paperwork taken care of and set up our appointment to get married. We have to wait forty-eight hours, something he wasn't happy about, but the clerk explained it was the law. Now? We're at a jewelry store and my jaw won't stay closed as Braxton has the sales girl bring out tray after tray of rings. He's looking for something specific for me so I leave him to it and head to the men's rings.

Another clerk comes up to me saying, "Can I help you?"

"Yes, I want to look at men's wedding bands. I have something particular in mind so hopefully you have it," I reply.

"Let me pull out some of the trays."

I'm so immersed in looking at the rings I don't hear Braxton come up behind me. I've narrowed it down to two of them, but need to know if it will match mine. "That one there, sweetheart, it'll go with yours almost perfectly," he whispers in my ear pointing at the one he wants.

Turning me, he lifts my left hand and slides the most gorgeous ring on my finger. It's a miner cut diamond surrounded by a band of smaller diamonds. "Oh, Braxton, it's gorgeous!" I whisper.

"The matching wedding band will allow it to fit in the middle."

Looking at my ring and the two that I was considering for him, I point to the one on the left and say, "That one, please." Thank goodness, it's the same one he selected!

"What size?"

Fuck if I know, I just know his fingers are big and they bring me a lot of pleasure everywhere they touch. *Focus Cara, dammit!* Looking at Braxton, I say, "You'll have to tell him that, honey."

"I wear a size eleven ring," Braxton tells the clerk.

"Do you want an inscription?"

"Yes, can you put 'You are my home, where I want to be' on it?

"Normally I wouldn't be able to do an inscription that large, but because of the size and width of the ring, it will fit just fine," the clerk says.

Braxton chuckles and I shoot him a look. He's so damn cocky sometimes, but if I'm being honest with myself, it's not in an arrogant, assholeish way, so it works for him.

Once we get the rings squared away, he takes me to grab something to eat before we head to the clubhouse. "Wait, what about the kids?" I know he mentioned it before but my pregnancy brain has me forgetting the simplest things these days!

"Sweetheart, I called Mom. She, your brother and parents are all good. We need this time, just the two of us."

"Even with Luca hurt?" I ask.

"Cara, even though we're both coming into this relationship with kids, at the end of the day, it's just going to be you and me. We have to make sure we have a solid foundation, and that means we have to have time with one another with no kids and no distractions."

I think about what he's saying and realize that he's right. We do need 'us' time, uninterrupted from the kids. And with all that we did today, we've got a lot to talk about. "Yeah, I agree."

Braxton

Laying in my bed at the clubhouse with Cara curled up in my arms, I think about what's coming up. I can't believe that I'll be a husband within the next few days, and have an old lady. Not to mention, the baby that's on the way. I guess some dreams are meant to come true, I know mine have.

Three days later, I find myself standing in front of the Justice of the Peace with Cara at my side. She wanted this small and intimate, so the only guests with us today are Mom, Lily, and Luca—wheelchair and all, and of course Ralynn since her mom is still out of town packing up their house.

Cara looks breathtaking in her white colored, simple spaghetti strap summer dress, the only reason I know that much is because I heard Mom and Cara talking about what kind of dress she was wearing. And something about ballet slippers, I was a little concerned at first, because when you think about those shoes you think of those bitches up on their toes. And there was no way in hell I was letting her leave the house in those contraptions. She'd break her fucking neck, not to mention look ridiculous.

"Do you, Braxton Callahan, take Caraleigh Jensen's hand in marriage? Do you promise to love, honor and protect her against all those who wish to do her harm?" The Judge looks over at me funny, yeah I wrote that shit. His only job is to read it not to judge me.

"I do."

"Caraleigh Jensen, do you take Braxton Callahan's hand in marriage? Do you promise to love, honor and cherish your marriage and family?" Once again he lifts his head from his notes to look at me in astonishment. What? She said no obey in our vows, I'm only honoring her wishes.

"I do," she says with a chuckle as she looks over and smiles at me.

"Braxton, repeat these vows after me," the Judge says to me.

"Before these witnesses here with us today, I vow to love you and care for you as long as we both shall live." I repeat what he says.

255

"I take you, with all your faults and strengths, as I offer myself to you with all my faults and strengths." Once again I repeat after him. "I will help you when you need help, and turn to you when I need help. I choose you as the person with whom I will spend my life." After I say these vows to Cara, I slip her ring on her finger.

Next Cara repeats the same vows and places my ring on my finger. I breathe a sigh of relief at having my ring on her finger and her having my last name...finally. We are waiting for Hatch and DJ to get back to have the cut ceremony, we both want all of our closest friends and family at our sides. I turn to Luca in his wheelchair and let him in on the other surprise we have awaiting today.

"Luca, today I not only take your mother as my wife, but you as my son. These papers here are legal adoption papers that the Judge will sign if you accept me as your dad...legally."

"Yeth!" he screams out causing us all to laugh, I look up at my girl and she has tears falling from her eyes. I'd worry except I know they're happy tears.

Cara leans down to Lily and tells her she has the same papers, but for her to be Lily's Mom. My baby girls breaks down and falls into Cara's arms. Mom has a handkerchief in hand and it's a good thing too because it's getting a lot of use.

The Judge signs both sets of adoption papers and announces out loud, "I'd like to introduce you to the Callahan family!" Mom cheers out loud causing the kids to break out into laughter.

Best day of my life, other than the day Lily was born...so far.

EPILOGUE

DJ

I'm so excited for Cara. And if I'm being honest, for myself as well. I never expected to meet someone like Hatch. We've been having a lot of fun and he's been good for me and Ralynn. Getting this house packed up is another story though. My book is with my beta readers and I'm dying to see what their feedback is so I can make changes and get it off to my editor.

The only wrinkle in everything is that bitch Starla. From what Cara has said, she flirts unmercilessly with Braxton because she's trying to get Hatch's attention. There's no way some bleach slut Barbie wannabe is gonna get my man!

Another thing weighing on my mind is, who in the hell contacted her in-laws from hell and informed them that Luca was in the hospital? It's a mystery that I intend to solve, and when I do that person better hope and pray that I am not the one to get hands on them first! Whoever they are, they have no idea about the wrath that is headed their way. No one messes with my family and is able to talk about it the next day. I have a mission, and I'm not taking it lightly.

Until that day comes, I intend to stand by my friends and enjoy this journey life has handed me on a silver platter...Hatchet.

The end.... for now!

Want to be present for Cara's cut ceremony?
Want to find out who told Mr. and Mrs. Jensen that Luca was in the hospital?
Want to find out what happens with the school and the kids being hurt?

These questions and more will be answered in Hatchet's book. Book 2 of the Rebel Guardians MC coming soon...

ABOUT LIBERTY

Liberty has been an avid reader for most of her life. When she was younger she used to sit and fill spiral notebooks full of stories for her grandmother. As she got older, she took the jobs needed for raising her boys as a single mom until she met her amazing husband. She has stopped working in the last few years and started off by promoting authors, then she took up blogging and reviewing for authors. This has led her down the path of writing and creating characters and telling their stories. She loves getting creative and working behind the scenes with her characters and bringing her imagination to life.

Find me on Facebook:
https://www.facebook.com/authorlibertyparker/?ref=bookmark

OTHER WORKS BY

LIBERTY

 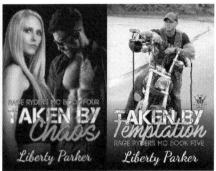

Current Standalones
What Should've Been
Charlee's Choices

ABOUT DARLENE

I am a transplanted Yankee, moving from upstate New York when I was a teenager. I live with the brat-cat pack and a small muffin dog, all rescues, as I plot and plan who will get to "talk" next!

Find me on Facebook!
https://www.facebook.com/darlenetallmanauthor

OTHER WORKS BY

DARLENE

Mischief Kitties
Co-written with Cherry Shephard and Alex J.:
The Mischief Kitties in Bampires & Ghosts &
New Friends Oh My!
The Mischief Kitties in The Great Glitter Caper

Standalones
Want to read my books?
"Bountiful Harvest"
"His Firefly"
"His Christmas Pixie"
"Her Kinsman-Redeemer"
"Operation Valentine"
"His Forever"

"Forgiveness"
"Reese Black Tuxedoes MC
"Christmas With Dixie"

By:
Liberty Parker
&
Darlene Tallman

COPYRIGHT

Hatchet
Rebel Guardians MC Novel
Copyright © Liberty Parker
& Darlene Tallman 2018
Published by Liberty Parker
& Darlene Tallman
Cover by: Dark Water Covers
https://goo.gl/mhVY1Y
Edited by: Joanne Dearman, Kat Beecham, Melanie
Grey, Jenni Belanger, Darlene Tallman
Formatting by: Liberty Parker

authorlibertyparker@yahoo.com
ddean228@yahoo.com

SYNOPSIS

Jayden "Hatchet" Hatcher is the Enforcer for the Rebel Guardians MC. He hides his past behind jokes, and will do anything for the brothers he has now. Life is good with easy women and plenty of fun. Until she walks into the barbeque that fateful summer weekend.

Donna Jo "DJ" Feldman is a single mom to Ralynn. On her own since she found out she was pregnant, she has a handful of people she trusts implicitly, including her best friend, Caraleigh Jenson. When she goes to visit Cara and meets the man they call Hatch, she realizes that life is too short not to reach for the brass ring.

What started out as a bit of fun soon turns into so much more for the two of them. But Hatch has unknown skeletons and when they come calling, will what DJ feels for him be enough? Can they survive with the love they have for one another and with their Rebel Guardians family at their back?

CHAPTER ONE

DJ

Present Day

Finally! The house is packed and I can get home to my little girl. As Hatchet pulls up with the moving van a wave of excitement fills me. I'm starting a new life away from this podunk town with the man I love and my daughter at my side. I haven't told Hatchet that I love him yet, I'm nervous that he may not be riding the same 'L' train as me. His actions speak that of love, but as a woman I can tell someone has hurt him in the past, and he's not quite ready to go down that road again. Don't get me wrong, as I said before, he shows me every day that I mean the world to him, the way his body moves when we're being intimate, the way he gets my coffee for me every morning to help me function—yes, he knows exactly how I take my cup of java. He's even given me some very erotic massages here lately when my body feels like it's full of knots and I can barely move. He calls my daughter every night with me to tell her goodnight, he even picks up small things for her when he sees them, always asking me if I think she'll like it. She loves Hatch just as much as I do, and I can't wait to see the excitement on her face when he gives her these small, thoughtful treasures.

Watching him back up, I can't help but be grateful that we hired some men for extra muscle, I didn't realize how much I had acquired while living in my home. It would take days for just Hatch and me to load the van, at least this way we can get it done in a day and be back on the road by nightfall. Hatch needs to get back to work, and I have a little girl that's none to happy that her mother has been away for as long as I have been.

"Hey, lover, glad you're back. I've got breakfast ready," I tell him, standing on my tiptoes for a kiss. I'm not exactly short at five feet six inches, but he still towers over me and makes me feel as tiny as a porcelain doll. He's built, with muscles that have muscles, and tattoos that span his arms and back, including the Rebel Guardians patch that's inked on his front right pec.

"We should have enough time to eat then. My old Army buddies will be here within the next two hours. May even be able to fit in a quickie," he replies, smirking at me. As if I'd protest a quickie! He knows me better than that, all he has to do is give me a certain look and I'm ready to climb his body and rip off his clothes.

"You know it," I tell him. He starts laughing at me, because according to him and the conversations we've had in the past...all I have to do is be in the same room with him and he's ready to throw me down and have his way with me...regardless of if anyone is in the room with us or not. One time, Ralynn walked in on us making out, she's never seen me with a man before and the shock on her face at seeing us will forever be ingrained in my brain.

"OOOHHH Momma that's nasty, why are you letting him suck your face," she said to me.

To which I replied, "Because I really like him."

"I'm never gonna let a boy suck my face like that," she told us.

"Better not," Hatchet told her.

"Hey, whatcha thinking about over there gorgeous?" he asks me.

"I was thinking about the time Ralynn caught us kissing."

"Yeah, that was hysterical."

"No it wasn't! She thought you were sucking my face Hatchet."

"What I remember is her saying no boy was going to do that to her, made me a happy man to know I won't be teaching any boys some lessons."

Him saying that makes my insides all warm and fuzzy, that he's planning to be around for the long-haul. Gotta say, I talk a good game, but honestly? It had been a long drought. Like, since I got pregnant with Ralynn. And it's not like he was the first good-looking man I was introduced to, but he was the first one who set me on fire with his teasing, his glances and his innocent touches. Thank goodness, they're not so innocent any longer, my vibrator was getting a workout! Plus, he doesn't care that I write steamy romance novels. In fact, he said I could use him for inspiration any time I wanted and if we had to research any positions, he was the man for the job. See why I love him?

He supports me and my career, he hasn't left my side for a long period of time since we made love the first time. He leaves, goes to work and comes back to Cara's apartment to spend the night with us. He spends a lot of time with Ralynn and Luca and they love him dearly. I even caught him once playing babies and I swear if I'd had my phone on me it would be full of pictures from that day alone. I barely have enough time in the day to sit and play with her, but somehow he makes the time and he even calls her his little princess. When he calls her that, her little face lights up, I never knew she was missing male attention, she's never asked about her father and I've never been forthcoming where he's concerned.

He wasn't a good man towards the end of our relationship, and as soon as he found out I was pregnant with Ralynn he hit the road without a backwards glance. I haven't heard from or seen him since that day, he never even called to find out if he has a son or daughter...the bastard. It's blank on her birth certificate where it asks the name of the father. He didn't deserve the right to be listed as far as I was concerned. I'm finding out, though, being around Hatch's brothers, that they take family seriously. I mean, look at Braxton. Not only does he have Lily, but he's gonna marry my bestie and she has a little boy and they're pregnant! Plus, Twisted and Paisley have a little boy, Tig. Ray is finally getting more kids to play with, something that was hard when Cara moved away. Not that she got to see Luca that much, especially during the last six months of Graham's life.

Now there's another douche nozzle! I hated what Cara had become being married to him. She's always been somewhat sassy and feisty but Graham and his parents? They constantly put her down and made her feel like shit so she stopped offering her opinion and started apologizing for everything. Glad to see she's back. Braxton's been good for her.

I like the old Cara with some added new spark. She's finally laughing and smiling again and not hiding behind the shell she'd formed in order to deal with that family. I call them the family from hell...because that's exactly what they are. I've always wondered if they have hidden horns underneath their hair. Lord only knows I've seen the evil that lurks inside of Mrs. Jenson a time or two. She never intimidated me though, I wasn't married to her piece of shit son, so I was never as accommodating to their whims as Cara was. She tried a few times to put me down, that shit didn't slide with me so I had to put her in her place.

Needless to say, I was never again invited back to their house, no skin off my back, but I felt bad that Cara had to deal with them and all of their socialite friends without having her girl at her back. If I could've slayed those dragons for her I would've, but some type of divine intervention happened and now she shouldn't have to deal with them since Graham is gone.

Alas, they showed up at Luca's hospital room, it's a good thing that I wasn't there because I would've grabbed the she-devil by the hair and dragged her from the room kicking and screaming all the way to the parking lot.There is no love lost between that family and me, I've never been a kiss-ass and I definitely will never start with those two.

"Now where'd you go?" Hatch asks me breaking me out of my thoughts.

"I'm thinking about those assholes showing up at Luca's room in the hospital."

"Gorgeous, let's concentrate on what we can do and not on something we can't do anything about. I'll make you a deal, let's get this done...get home, get unloaded, get a good night's rest and then you can do your sleuth thing."

"My sleuth thing?"

"Yes, I know you and I'm aware of the fact that you want to get home and investigate how those two found out Luca was in the hospital."

"You know me well, huh?"

"I pay attention to anything that has to do with you baby, now let's get that quickie in shall we?"

"Did you even eat breakfast yet?"

"Sure did, ate all of it like a big boy while you were lost in thought."

"Lead the way then, I know we have our mattress on the floor still in the bedroom."

"Mattress, who needs a mattress when there's a perfectly good wall there," he says pointing to the wall off the kitchen that is bare of boxes and pictures. "Or, the kitchen table, the floor...use your imagination woman. We are not the vanilla plain jane type of people DJ," he says while scooping me up in his arms and laying a kiss on my lips.

Well, I used to be a vanilla girl, but Hatch has brought a side of me out that even makes me blush! I grin at him as he deposits me on the kitchen table and then immediately slips my leggings and panties down my legs before tossing them aside. "Now? I get some dessert," he says before he lowers his mouth to my aching core.

"Um, dessert is generally eaten after a dinner meal," I tell him, giggling.

"I have a bit of a sweet tooth, darlin', remember? And right now, I need your special sweetness."

"As long as you don't stop what you're doing right now, I'm not gonna complain," I say, the last words coming out breathier than normal because he added two fingers to the mix. "Fuck, Hatch, I'm gonna come if you keep that up."

"That's the plan, gorgeous. First my tongue and fingers, then my cock."

He's not wasting time, likely so his dick can get in on the action but trust me, I am not complaining one bit. Without warning, my orgasm hits and I scream, my fingers searching for something to hang onto as I feel like I'm floating away. A slap to the outside of my thigh has me lifting my head. "Need you bent over the table, woman," he says, already lowering his jeans down his magnificent ass and thighs.

Seeing how hard he is, I quickly flip myself over and scoot down so my feet are touching the floor. I feel him gently spread my legs further and a quiver settles deep inside because I know how it's going to feel when he moves in me - fucking heaven. "You ready, gorgeous?" he asks as he moves his cock through my folds.

"Mmhmm," I mumble out, still a bit out of it from the wicked orgasm I just had.

With a powerful thrust, he's buried balls deep in me and the stretch and burn is one that is pleasurable. I've never been one to worry about a man's size, figuring that if they know how to use it, that's all that matters, but Hatch? That man is blessed in the dick department! His grip on my hips tightens as he begins moving in and out of me and I feel myself trying to push back against him. The

279

table might be the perfect height for him to fuck me, but it sucks for me because I have no real traction to move.

"I got this gorgeous," he says, "you just relax."

Relax? Is he out of his fucking mind? He's got me close to orgasm number two for the morning for heaven's sake! Shit, now he's changed angles or something and is hitting..." Hatch!" I shriek as orgasm number two shatters me in two.

Hatch

Ah having this woman pretty much helpless as I thrust into her is such a fucking turn on I have been doing what I could to hold back. When I feel her pussy squeezing the life out of my dick, however, I can't hold off any longer and with a shout, I call out her name as I empty myself into her wet, warm sheath. Fuck, she's the best I've ever had. And her feisty, take no shit attitude? Hell, if I'm honest I got hard the first time I heard her giving our prospect shit the day she showed up at the barbeque.

"C'mon gorgeous, let's get you cleaned up before the guys get here."

"M'kay."

I help her stand up and my ego jacks up another notch seeing her wobbly and unsteady. After

Anniston's betrayal, I've stayed away from relationships, but damn, DJ has everything in spades that I want in a woman—she's independent, a helluva good mom, attractive, and fucking sexy as hell. With the way I feel, I know that if she gained two hundred pounds, I'd still be panting after her like a dog in heat. She heads off to the bathroom finally, throwing a smirk at me over her shoulder and I'm about to go smack that sassy ass swaying in front of me when I hear a knock at the door. I wait until I hear the click of the bathroom door before I head to the door and open it up.

"Hey y'all, appreciate you being able to help my woman out."

"Not a problem," Joey says, stepping inside.

"Always glad to help," Carlton replies.

"Doesn't look like it'll take us too long," Jorge states.

"Naw, and there's a hand-truck in the back of the trailer," I tell them. DJ is a bit OCD and has labeled each box with the basic contents and room, so it will be easy to get it on the truck. The only thing left is the bedding and she threw that in the washer when we first got up so it would be 'clean' when we got there and unloaded. I know it's gonna be a long ass day, but honestly? I can't wait to get home and see my little princess. Yeah, I know she's not my kid, however, her genuine affection towards me has made me fall love with her. And her mom. Although it's too soon to tell DJ that because from

281

what little she's shared, she's been shit on a lot in her life.

As Jorge goes out to get the hand-truck so we can start loading, my mind drifts back to the first night we spent together.

"I'm not usually like this," she said.

"What do you mean?"

"I mean, sleeping with someone on the first date."

"Never took you for easy, darlin', but I know you feel the connection we've got."

She sighed before sitting up on the bed and looking down at me. "No, you don't understand Hatch. Ralynn's dad and I dated for about six months before I got pregnant. When I got pregnant, he split, never to be heard from again. He doesn't even know if I kept the baby or what I had for fuck's sake! Since then, my focus has been on finishing college while raising my baby girl. I've gone out on dates, but it never went very far."

I looked at her stunned. If I'm catching what she's saying, she hasn't had sex in a helluva long time. "So you haven't had sex since Ralynn was conceived?"

"No."

"Why me, babe?"

"Because I can talk to you, because you make my body quake with need, because you embody everything I've ever wanted in a man."

I pull her back down so we're facing one another, but barely touching. Cupping her face, I lean in and kiss her. It's not a hot and heavy, I want to fuck your brains out kiss. No, it's one filled with promise and need. Something about this woman has me thinking of forever for the first time in a long, long time. And that thought should scare the shit out of me but it doesn't.

"Hatch, your woman made sure we would know where shit went, huh?" Carlton asks, breaking me out of my thoughts.

"Yeah. In fact, she has boxes for the bedroom, bathroom and kitchen marked 'put in last' so that when we get there and unload, she can get those unpacked first."

"Damn, she's organized."

"You have no idea."

This is unedited and subject to change as the story progresses. I hope you enjoyed a sneak peek into Hatch and DJ's story.